GRANTA BOOKS

HAROUN AND THE SEA OF STORIES

Salman Rushdie

Haroun and the Sea of Stories

GRANTA BOOKS
LONDON
in association with
PENGUIN BOOKS

GRANTA BOOKS
2/3 Hanover Yard, Noel Road, Islington, London N1 8BE

Published in association with the Penguin Group
Penguin Books Ltd, 27 Wrights Lane, London W8 5TZ, England
Viking Penguin, a division of Penguin Books USA Inc.,
375 Hudson Street, New York 10014, USA
Penguin Books Australia Ltd, Ringwood, Victoria, Australia
Penguin Books Canada Ltd, 2801 John Street, Markham,
Ontario, Canada L3R 1B4
Penguin Books (NZ) Ltd, 182-190 Wairau Road,
Auckland 10, New Zealand

Penguin Books Ltd, Registered Offices: Harmondsworth,
Middlesex, England

First published 1990

1 3 5 7 9 10 8 6 4 2

Printed in England

A CIP catalogue record for this book is available from
the British Library

ISBN 0-14-014223-1

CONTENTS

Z embla, Zenda, Xanadu:
A ll our dream-worlds may come true.
F airy lands are fearsome too.
A s I wander far from view
R ead, and bring me home to you.

1

The Shah of Blah

There was once, in the country of Alifbay, a sad city, the saddest of cities, a city so ruinously sad that it had forgotten its name. It stood by a mournful sea full of glumfish, which were so miserable to eat that they made people belch with melancholy even though the skies were blue.

In the north of the sad city stood mighty factories in which (so I'm told) sadness was actually manufactured, packaged and sent all over the world, which never seemed to get enough of it. Black smoke poured out of the chimneys of the sadness factories and hung over the city like bad news.

And in the depths of the city, beyond an old zone of ruined buildings that looked like broken hearts, there lived a happy young fellow by the name of Haroun, the only child of the storyteller Rashid Khalifa, whose cheerfulness was famous throughout that unhappy metropolis, and whose never-ending stream of tall, short and winding tales had earned him not one but two nicknames. To his admirers he was Rashid the Ocean of Notions, as stuffed with cheery stories as the sea was full of glumfish; but to his jealous rivals he was the Shah of Blah. To his wife, Soraya, Rashid was for many years as loving a husband as anyone could wish for, and during these years Haroun grew up in a home in which, instead of misery and frowns, he had his father's ready laughter and his mother's sweet voice raised in song.

Then something went wrong. (Maybe the sadness of the city finally crept in through their windows.)

The day Soraya stopped singing, in the middle of a line, as

if someone had thrown a switch, Haroun guessed there was trouble brewing. But he never suspected how much.

~ ~ ~

Rashid Khalifa was so busy making up and telling stories that he didn't notice that Soraya no longer sang; which probably made things worse. But then Rashid was a busy man, in constant demand, he was the Ocean of Notions, the famous Shah of Blah. And what with all his rehearsals and performances, Rashid was so often on stage that he lost track of what was going on in his own home. He sped around the city and the country telling stories, while Soraya stayed home, turning cloudy and even a little thunderous and brewing up quite a storm.

Haroun went with his father whenever he could, because the man was a magician, it couldn't be denied. He would climb up on to some little makeshift stage in a dead-end alley packed with raggedy children and toothless old-timers, all squatting in the dust; and once he got going even the city's many wandering cows would stop and cock their ears, and monkeys would jabber approvingly from rooftops and the parrots in the trees would imitate his voice.

Haroun often thought of his father as a Juggler, because his stories were really lots of different tales juggled together, and Rashid kept them going in a sort of dizzy whirl, and never made a mistake.

Where did all these stories come from? It seemed that all Rashid had to do was to part his lips in a plump red smile and out would pop some brand-new saga, complete with sorcery, love-interest, princesses, wicked uncles, fat aunts, mustachioed gangsters in yellow check pants, fantastic locations, cowards, heroes, fights, and half a dozen catchy, hummable tunes. 'Everything comes from somewhere,' Haroun reasoned, 'so these stories can't simply come out of thin air . . . ?'

But whenever he asked his father this most important of questions, the Shah of Blah would narrow his (to tell the truth) slightly bulging eyes, and pat his wobbly stomach, and stick his thumb between his lips while he made ridiculous drinking noises, *glug glug glug*. Haroun hated it when his father acted this way. 'No, come on, where do they come from really?' he'd insist, and Rashid would wiggle his eyebrows mysteriously and make witchy fingers in the air.

'From the great Story Sea,' he'd reply. 'I drink the warm Story Waters and then I feel full of steam.'

Haroun found this statement intensely irritating. 'Where do you keep this hot water, then?' he argued craftily. 'In hot-water bottles, I suppose. Well, I've never seen any.'

'It comes out of an invisible Tap installed by one of the Water Genies,' said Rashid with a straight face. 'You have to be a subscriber.'

'And how do you become a subscriber?'

'Oh,' said the Shah of Blah, 'that's much Too Complicated To Explain.'

'Anyhow,' said Haroun grumpily, 'I've never seen a Water Genie, either.' Rashid shrugged. 'You're never up in time to see the milkman,' he pointed out, 'but you don't mind drinking the milk. So now kindly desist from this Iffing and Butting and be happy with the stories you enjoy.' And that was the end of that.

Except that one day Haroun asked one question too many, and then all hell broke loose.

~ ~ ~

The Khalifas lived in the downstairs part of a small concrete house with pink walls, lime-green windows and blue-painted balconies with squiggly metal railings, all of which made it look (in Haroun's view) more like a cake than a building. It wasn't a grand house, nothing like the skyscrapers where the super-rich folks lived; then again, it was nothing like the dwellings of the poor, either. The poor lived in tumbledown shacks made of old cardboard boxes and plastic sheeting, and these shacks were glued together by despair. And then there were the super-poor, who had no homes at all. They slept on pavements and in the doorways of shops, and had to pay rent to local gangsters for doing even that. So the truth is that Haroun was lucky; but luck has a way of running out without the slightest warning. One minute you've got a lucky star watching over you and the next instant it's done a bunk.

~ ~ ~

In the sad city, people mostly had big families; but the poor children got sick and starved, while the rich kids overate and quarrelled over their parents' money. Still Haroun wanted to know why his parents hadn't had more children, but the only answer he ever got from Rashid was no answer at all:

'There's more to you, young Haroun Khalifa, than meets the blinking eye.'

Well, what was *that* supposed to mean? 'We used up our full quota of child-stuff just in making you,' Rashid explained. 'It's all packed in there, enough for maybe four-five kiddies. Yes, sir, more to you than the blinking eye can see.'

Straight answers were beyond the powers of Rashid Khalifa, who would never take a short cut if there was a longer, twistier road available. Soraya gave Haroun a simpler reply. 'We tried,' she sadly said. 'This child business is not such an easy thing. Think of the poor Senguptas.'

The Senguptas lived upstairs. Mr Sengupta was a clerk at the offices of the City Corporation and he was as sticky-thin and whiny-voiced and mingy as his wife Oneeta was generous and loud and wobbly-fat. They had no children at all, and as a result Oneeta Sengupta paid more attention to Haroun than he really cared for. She brought him sweetmeats (which was fine), and ruffled his hair (which wasn't), and when she hugged him the great cascades of her flesh seemed to surround him completely, to his considerable alarm.

Mr Sengupta ignored Haroun, but was always talking to Soraya, which Haroun didn't like, particularly as the fellow would launch into criticisms of Rashid the storyteller whenever he thought Haroun wasn't listening. 'That husband of yours, excuse me if I mention,' he would start in his thin whiny voice. 'He's got his head stuck in the air and his feet off the ground. What are all these stories? Life is not a storybook or joke shop. All this fun will come to no good. What's the use of stories that aren't even true?'

Haroun, listening hard outside the window, decided he did not care for Mr Sengupta, this man who hated stories and storytellers: he didn't care for him one little bit.

What's the use of stories that aren't even true? Haroun couldn't get the terrible question out of his head. However, there were people who thought Rashid's stories were useful. In those days it was almost election time, and the Grand Panjandrums of various political parties all came to Rashid, smiling their fat-cat smiles, to beg him to tell his stories at their rallies and nobody else's. It was well known that if you could get Rashid's magic tongue on your side then your troubles were over. Nobody ever believed anything a politico said, even though they pretended as hard as they could that they were telling the truth. (In fact, this was how everyone knew they were lying.) But everyone had complete faith in Rashid, because he always admitted that everything he told them was completely untrue and made up out of his own head. So the politicos needed Rashid to help them win the people's votes. They lined up outside his door with their shiny faces and fake smiles and bags of hard cash. Rashid could pick and choose.

~ ~ ~

On the day that everything went wrong, Haroun was on his way home from school when he was caught in the first downpour of the rainy season.

Now, when the rains came to the sad city, life became a little easier to bear. There were delicious pomfret in the sea at that time of year, so people could have a break from the glumfish; and the air was cool and clean, because the rain washed away most of the black smoke billowing out of the sadness factories. Haroun Khalifa loved the feeling of getting soaked to the skin in the first rain of the year, so he skipped about and got a wonderful warm drenching, and opened his mouth to let the raindrops plop on to his tongue. He arrived home looking as wet and shiny as a pomfret in the sea.

Miss Oneeta was standing on her upstairs balcony, shaking like a jelly; and if it hadn't been raining, Haroun might have noticed that she was crying. He went indoors and found Rashid the storyteller looking as if he'd stuck his face out of the window, because his eyes and cheeks were soaking wet, even though his clothes were dry.

Haroun's mother, Soraya, had run off with Mr Sengupta.

At eleven a.m. precisely, she had sent Rashid into Haroun's room, telling him to search for some missing socks. A few seconds later, while he was busy with the hunt (Haroun was good at losing socks), Rashid heard the front door slam, and, an instant later, the sound of a car in the lane. He returned to the living room to find his wife gone, and a taxi speeding away around the corner. 'She must have planned it all very carefully,' he thought. The clock still stood at eleven o'clock exactly. Rashid picked up a hammer and smashed the clock to bits. Then he broke every other clock in the house, including the one on Haroun's bedside table.

The first thing Haroun said on hearing the news of his

mother's departure was, 'What did you have to break my clock for?'

Soraya had left a note full of all the nasty things Mr Sengupta used to say about Rashid: 'You are only interested in pleasure, but a proper man would know that life is a serious business. Your brain is full of make-believe, so there is no room in it for facts. Mr Sengupta has no imagination at all. This is okay by me.' There was a postscript. 'Tell Haroun I love him, but I can't help it, I have to do this now.'

Rainwater dripped on to the note from Haroun's hair. 'What to do, son,' Rashid pleaded piteously. 'Storytelling is the only work I know.'

When he heard his father sounding so pathetic, Haroun lost his temper and shouted: 'What's the point of it? *What's the use of stories that aren't even true?*'

Rashid hid his face in his hands and wept.

Haroun wanted to get those words back, to pull them out of his father's ears and shove them back into his own mouth; but of course he couldn't do that. And that was why he blamed himself when, soon afterwards and in the most embarrassing circumstances imaginable, an Unthinkable Thing happened:

Rashid Khalifa, the legendary Ocean of Notions, the fabled Shah of Blah, stood up in front of a huge audience, opened his mouth, and found that he had run out of stories to tell.

~ ~ ~

After his mother left home, Haroun found that he couldn't keep his mind on anything for very long, or, to be precise, for more than eleven minutes at a time. Rashid took him to a movie to cheer him up, but after exactly eleven minutes Haroun's attention wandered, and when the film ended he had no idea how it all turned out, and had to ask Rashid if the good guys won in the end. The next day Haroun was playing goalie in a neighbourhood game of street hockey, and after pulling off a string of brilliant saves in the first eleven minutes he began to let in the softest, most foolish and most humiliating of goals. And so it went on: his mind was always wandering off somewhere and leaving his body behind. This created certain difficulties, because many interesting and some important things take longer than eleven minutes: meals, for example, and also mathematics examinations.

It was Oneeta Sengupta who put her finger on the trouble. She had started coming downstairs even more often than before, for instance to announce defiantly: 'No more Mrs Sengupta for me! From today, call me Miss Oneeta only!'—after which she smacked her forehead violently, and wailed: 'O! O! What is to become?'

When Rashid told Miss Oneeta about Haroun's wandering attention, however, she spoke firmly and with certainty. 'Eleven o'clock when his mother exited,' she declared. 'Now comes this problem of eleven minutes.

Cause is located in his pussy-collar-jee.' It took Rashid and Haroun a few moments to work out that she meant *psychology*. 'Owing to pussy-collar-jeecal sadness,' Miss Oneeta continued, 'the young master is stuck fast on his eleven number and cannot get to twelve.'

'That's not true,' Haroun protested; but in his heart he feared it might be. Was he stuck in time like a broken clock? Maybe the problem would never be solved unless and until Soraya returned to start the clocks up once again.

~ ~ ~

Some days later Rashid Khalifa was invited to perform by politicos from the Town of G and the nearby Valley of K, which nestled in the Mountains of M. (I should explain that in the country of Alifbay many places were named after letters of the Alphabet. This led to much confusion, because there were only a limited number of letters and an almost unlimited number of places in need of names. As a result many places were obliged to share a single name. This meant that people's letters were always going to the wrong address. Such difficulties were made even worse by the way in which certain places, such as the sad city, forgot their names entirely. The employees of the national mail service had a lot to put up with, as you can imagine, so they could get a little excitable on occasion.)

'We should go,' Rashid said to Haroun, putting a brave face on things. 'In the Town of G and the Valley of K, the weather is still fine; whereas here the air is too weepy for words.'

It was true that it was raining so hard in the sad city that you could almost drown just by breathing in. Miss Oneeta, who just happened to have dropped in from upstairs, agreed sadly with Rashid. 'Tip-top plan,' she said. 'Yes, both of you, go; it will be like a little holiday, and no need to worry about me, sitting sitting all by myself.'

~ ~ ~

'The Town of G is not so special,' Rashid told Haroun as the train carried them towards that very place. 'But the Valley of K! Now that is different. There are fields of gold and mountains of silver and in the middle of the Valley there is a beautiful Lake whose name, by the way, is Dull.'

'If it's so beautiful, why isn't it called Interesting?' Haroun argued; and Rashid, making a huge effort to be in a good mood, tried to put on his old witchy-fingers act. 'Ah—now—the *Interesting* Lake,' he said in his most mysterious voice. 'Now that's something else again. That's a Lake of Many Names, yes, sir, so it is.'

Rashid went on trying to sound happy. He told Haroun about the Luxury Class Houseboat waiting for them on the Dull Lake. He talked about the ruined fairy castle in the silver mountains, and about the pleasure gardens built by the ancient Emperors, which came right down to the edge of the Dull Lake: gardens with fountains and terraces and pavilions of pleasure, where the spirits of the ancient kings still flew about in the guise of hoopoe birds. But after exactly eleven minutes Haroun stopped listening; and Rashid stopped talking, too, and they stared silently out of

the window of the railway carriage at the unfolding
boredom of the plains.

They were met at the Railway Station in the Town of G
by two unsmiling men wearing gigantic mustachios and loud
yellow check pants. 'They look like villains to me,' Haroun
thought, but he kept his opinion to himself. The two men
drove Rashid and Haroun straight to the political rally. They
drove past buses that dripped people the way a sponge drips
water, and arrived at a thick forest of human beings, a crowd
of people sprouting in all directions like leaves on jungle
trees. There were great bushes of children and rows of ladies
arranged in lines, like flowers in a giant flower-bed. Rashid
was deep in his own thoughts, and was nodding sadly to
himself.

Then the thing happened, the Unthinkable Thing. Rashid
went out on to the stage in front of that vast jungle of a
crowd, and Haroun watched him from the wings—and the
poor storyteller opened his mouth, and the crowd squealed
in excitement—and now Rashid Khalifa, standing there
with his mouth hanging open, found that it was as empty as
his heart.

'Ark.' That was all that came out. The Shah of Blah
sounded like a stupid crow. 'Ark, ark, ark.'

~ ~ ~

After that they were shut up in a steaming hot office while
the two men with the mustachios and loud yellow check
pants shouted at Rashid and accused him of having taken a

bribe from their rivals, and suggested that they might cut off his tongue and other items also. —And Rashid, close to tears, kept repeating that he couldn't understand why he had dried up, and promising to make it up to them. 'In the Valley of K, I will be terrifico, magnifique,' he vowed.

'Better you are,' the mustachioed men shouted back. 'Or else, out comes that tongue from your lying throat.'

'So when does the plane leave for K?' Haroun butted in, hoping to calm things down. (The train, he knew, didn't go into the mountains.) The shouting men began to shout even more loudly. 'Plane? *Plane?* His papa's stories won't take off but the brat wants to fly! —No plane for you, mister and sonny. Catch a blasted bus.'

'My fault again,' Haroun thought wretchedly. 'I started all this off. *What's the use of stories that aren't even true.* I asked that question and it broke my father's heart. So it's up to me to put things right. Something has to be done.'

The only trouble was, he couldn't think of a single thing.

2

The Mail Coach

The two shouting men shoved Rashid and Haroun into the back seat of a beaten-up car with torn scarlet seats, and even though the car's cheap radio was playing movie music at top volume, the shouting men went on shouting about the unreliability of storytellers all the way to the rusting iron gates of the Bus Depot. Here Haroun and Rashid were dumped out of the car without ceremony or farewell.

'Expenses of the journey?' Rashid hopefully inquired, but the shouting men shouted, 'More cash demands! Cheek! Cheek of the chappie!' and drove away at high speed, forcing dogs and cows and women with baskets of fruit on their heads to dive out of the way. Loud music and rude words continued to pour out of the car as it zigzagged away into the distance.

Rashid didn't even bother to shake his fist. Haroun followed him towards the Ticket Office across a dusty courtyard with walls covered in strange warnings:

> IF YOU TRY TO RUSH OR ZOOM
> YOU ARE SURE TO MEET YOUR DOOM

was one of them, and

> ALL THE DANGEROUS OVERTAKERS
> END UP SAFE AT UNDERTAKER'S

was another, and also

> LOOK OUT! SLOW DOWN! DON'T BE FUNNY!
> LIFE IS PRECIOUS! CARS COST MONEY!

'There should be one about not shouting at the passengers in the back seat,' Haroun muttered. Rashid went to buy a ticket.

There was a wrestling match at the ticket window instead of a queue, because everyone wanted to be first; and as most people were carrying chickens or children or other bulky items, the result was a free-for-all out of which feathers and toys and dislodged hats kept flying. And from time to time some dizzy fellow with ripped clothes would burst out of the mêlée, triumphantly waving a little scrap of paper: his ticket! Rashid, taking a deep breath, dived into the scrum.

Meanwhile, in the courtyard of the buses, small dust-clouds were rushing back and forth like little desert whirlwinds. Haroun realized that these clouds were full of human beings. There were simply too many passengers at the Bus Depot to fit into the available buses, and, anyhow, nobody knew which bus was leaving first; which made it possible for the drivers to play a mischievous game. One driver would start his engine, adjust his mirrors, and behave as if he were about to leave. At once a bunch of passengers would gather up their suitcases and bedrolls and parrots and transistor radios and rush towards him. Then he'd switch off his engine with an innocent smile; while on the far side of the courtyard, a different bus would start up, and the passengers would start running all over again.

'It's not fair,' Haroun said aloud.

'Correct,' a booming voice behind him answered, 'but but but you'll admit it's too much fun to watch.'

The owner of this voice turned out to be an enormous

fellow with a great quiff of hair standing straight up on his head, like a parrot's crest. His face, too, was extremely hairy; and the thought popped into Haroun's mind that all this hair was, well, somehow *feather-like*. 'Ridiculous idea,' he told himself. 'What on earth made me think of a thing like that? It's just plain nonsense, as anyone can see.'

Just then two separate dust-clouds of scurrying passengers collided in an explosion of umbrellas and milk-churns and rope sandals, and Haroun, without meaning to, began to laugh. 'You're a tip-top type,' boomed the fellow with the feathery hair. 'You see the funny side! An accident is truly a sad and cruel thing, but but but—crash! Wham! Spatoosh!—how it makes one giggle and hoot.' Here the giant stood and bowed. 'At your service,' he said. 'My goodname is Butt, driver of the Number One Super Express Mail Coach to the Valley of K.' Haroun thought he should bow, too. 'And my, as you say, goodname is Haroun.'

Then he had an idea, and added: 'If you mean what you say about being at my service, then in fact there is something you can do.'

'It was a figure of speech,' Mr Butt replied. 'But but but I will stand by it! A figure of speech is a shifty thing; it can be twisted or it can be straight. But Butt's a straight man, not a twister. What's your wish, my young mister?'

Rashid had often told Haroun about the beauty of the road from the Town of G to the Valley of K, a road that climbed like a serpent through the Pass of H towards the Tunnel of I (which was also known as J). There was snow by the roadside, and there were fabulous multicoloured birds gliding in the gorges; and when the road emerged from the Tunnel (Rashid had said), then the traveller saw before him the most spectacular view on earth, a vista of the Valley of K with its golden fields and silver mountains and with the Dull Lake at its heart—a view spread out like a magic carpet, waiting for someone to come and take a ride. 'No man can be sad who looks upon that sight,' Rashid had said, 'but a blind man's blindness must feel twice as wretched then.' So what Haroun asked Mr Butt for was this: front-row seats in the Mail Coach all the way to the Dull Lake; and a guarantee that the Mail Coach would pass through the Tunnel of I (also known as J) before sunset, because otherwise the whole point would be lost.

'But but but,' Mr Butt protested, 'the hour is already late . . . ' Then, seeing Haroun's face begin to fall, he grinned broadly and clapped his hands. 'But but but so what?' he shouted. 'The beautiful view! To cheer up the sad dad! Before sunset! *No problem.*'

So when Rashid staggered out of the Ticket Office he found Haroun waiting on the steps of the Mail Coach, with the best seats reserved inside, and the motor running.

The other passengers, who were out of breath from their running, and who were covered in dust which their sweat was turning to mud, stared at Haroun with a mixture of jealousy and awe. Rashid was impressed, too. 'As I may have mentioned, young Haroun Khalifa: more to you than meets the blinking eye.'

'Yahoo!' yelled Mr Butt, who was as excitable as any mail service employee. 'Varoom!' he added, and jammed the accelerator pedal right down against the floor.

The Mail Coach rocketed through the gates of the Bus Depot, narrowly missing a wall on which Haroun read this:

IF FROM SPEED YOU GET YOUR THRILL
TAKE PRECAUTION—MAKE YOUR WILL

~ ~ ~

Faster and faster went the Mail Coach; the passengers started to hoot and howl with excitement and fear. Through village after village Mr Butt drove, at top speed. Haroun observed that in each village a man carrying a large mailbag would be waiting by the bus stop in the village square, and that this man would look at first confused and then furious as the Mail Coach roared by him without even slowing down. Haroun could also see that at the rear of the Mail Coach there was a special area, separated from the passengers by a wire mesh partition, that was piled high with mailbags just like those held by the angry, fist-shaking men in the village squares. Mr Butt had apparently forgotten to deliver or collect the mail!

'Don't we need to stop for the letters?' Haroun finally leant forward to inquire. At the same moment Rashid the storyteller cried out, 'Do we need to go so blinking fast?'

Mr Butt managed to make the Mail Coach go even faster. '"Need to stop?"' he bellowed over his shoulder. '"Need to go so quickly?" Well, my sirs, I'll tell you this: Need's a slippery snake, that's what it is. The boy here says that you, sir, Need A View Before Sunset, and maybe it's so and maybe no. And some might say that the boy here Needs A Mother, and maybe it's so and maybe no. And it's been said of me that Butt Needs Speed, but but but it may be that my heart truly needs a Different Sort Of Thrill. O, Need's a funny fish: it makes people untruthful. They all suffer from it, but they will not always admit. Hurrah!' he added, pointing. 'The snow line! Icy patches ahead! Crumbling road surface! Hairpin bends! Danger of avalanches! *Full speed ahead!*'

He had simply decided not to stop for the mail in order to keep his promise to Haroun. '*No problem*,' he shouted gaily. 'Everybody gets other people's correspondence anyhow in this country of so-many too-many places and so-few too-few names.' The Mail Coach rushed up into the Mountains of M, swinging around terrifying curves with a great squealing of tyres. The luggage (which was all tied down on the roof rack) began to shift about in a worrying way. The passengers (who all looked alike, now that their perspiration had finished turning the dust that covered them to mud) began to complain.

'My holdall!' yelled a mud-woman. 'Crazy buffalo! Looney tune! Desist from your speeding, or my possessions will be thrown to Kingdom Come!'

'It is we ourselves who will be thrown, madam,' a mud-man answered sharply. 'So less noise about your personal items, please.' He was interrupted angrily by a second mud-man: 'Have a care! It is my goodwife you are insulting!' Then a second mud-woman joined in: 'So what? For so long she has been shouting-shouting in my husband's goodear, so why should not he lodge complaint? See her, the dirty skinnybones. Is she a woman or a muddy stick?'

'See here, this bend, what a tight one!' Mr Butt sang out. 'Here, two weeks ago, occurred a major disaster. Bus plunged into gully, all persons killed, sixty-seventy lives minimum. God! Too sad! If you desire I can stop for taking of photographs.'

'Yes, stop, stop,' the passengers begged (anything to make him slow down), but Mr Butt went even faster instead. 'Too late,' he yodelled gaily. 'Already it is far behind. Requests must be more promptly made if I am to comply.'

'I did it again,' Haroun was thinking. 'If we crash now, if we're smashed to bits or fried like potato chips in a burning wreck, it will be my fault this time, too.'

~ ~ ~

Now they were high in the Mountains of M, and Haroun felt sure that the Mail Coach was speeding up as they got higher. They were so high that there were clouds in the gorges below them, and the mountainsides were covered in thick, dirty snow and the passengers were shivering with cold. The only sound to be heard in the Mail Coach was the chattering of teeth. Everyone had fallen into a scared and frozen silence, while Mr Butt was concentrating so hard on his high-speed driving that he had even stopped yelling 'Yahoo' and pointing out the sites of particularly gruesome accidents.

Haroun had the feeling that they were floating on a sea of silence, that a wave of silence was lifting them up, up, up towards the mountaintops. His mouth was dry and his tongue felt stiff and caked. Rashid couldn't make a sound either, not even *ark*. 'Any moment now,' Haroun was thinking—and he knew that something very similar must be in the mind of each passenger—'I am going to be wiped out, like a word on a blackboard, one swoosh of the duster and I'll be gone for good.'

Then he saw the cloud.

The Mail Coach was streaking along the side of a narrow ravine. Up ahead the road swung so sharply to the right that it seemed they must plunge over the edge. Roadside notices warned of the extra danger, in words so severe that they no longer rhymed. DRIVE LIKE HELL AND YOU WILL GET THERE was one, and also: BE DEAD SLOW OR BE DEAD. Just then a thick cloud, shot through with impossible, shifting colours, a cloud from a dream or a nightmare, hopped up from the gorge below them and plopped itself down on the road. They hit it just as they went round the bend, and in the sudden darkness Haroun heard Butt slamming on the brakes as hard as he could.

Noise returned: screams, the skidding of tyres. 'This is it,' Haroun thought—and then they were out of the cloud, in a place with smooth walls curving up around them, and rows of yellow lights set in the ceiling above.

'Tunnel,' Mr Butt announced. 'At the far end, Valley of K. Hours to sunset, one. Time in tunnel, some minutes only. One View coming up. Like I said: *no problem.*'

~ ~ ~

They came out of the Tunnel of I, and Mr Butt stopped the Mail Coach so that everyone could enjoy the sight of the sun setting over the Valley of K, with its fields of gold (which really grew saffron) and its silver mountains (which were really covered in glistening, pure, white snow) and its Dull Lake (which didn't look dull at all). Rashid Khalifa hugged Haroun and said, 'Thanks for fixing this up, son, but I admit that for some time I thought we were all fixed good and proper, I mean done for, finito, *khattam-shud*.'

'Khattam-Shud,' Haroun frowned. 'What was that story you used to tell . . . ?'

Rashid spoke as if he were remembering an old, old dream.

'Khattam-Shud,' he said slowly, 'is the Arch-Enemy of all Stories, even of Language itself. He is the Prince of Silence and the Foe of Speech. And because everything ends, because dreams end, stories end, life ends, at the finish of everything we use his name. "It's finished," we tell one another, "it's over. Khattam-Shud: The End." '

'This place is already doing you good,' Haroun noted. 'No more *ark*. Your crazy stories are starting to come back.'

On the way down into the Valley, Mr Butt drove slowly and with extreme caution. 'But but but there is no Need for Speed now that my service has been performed,' he explained to the quivering mud-men and mud-women, who then all glared furiously at Haroun and Rashid.

As the light failed, they passed a sign that had originally

read WELCOME TO K; but somebody had daubed it with crude, irregular letters, so that it now said WELCOME TO KOSH-MAR.

'What's Kosh-Mar?' Haroun wanted to know.

'It's the work of some miscreant,' shrugged Mr Butt. 'Not every person in the Valley is happy, as you may find.'

'It's a word from the ancient tongue of Franj, which is no longer spoken in these parts,' Rashid explained. 'In those long-gone days the Valley, which is now simply K, had other names. One, if I remember correctly, was "Kache-Mer". Another was this "Kosh-Mar".'

'Do those names mean anything?' Haroun asked.

'All names mean something,' Rashid replied. 'Let me think. Yes, that was it. "Kache-Mer" can be translated as "the place that hides a Sea". But "Kosh-Mar" is a ruder name.'

'Come on,' urged Haroun. 'You can't stop there.'

'In the old tongue,' Rashid admitted, 'it was the word for "nightmare".'

~ ~ ~

It was dark when the Mail Coach arrived at the Bus Depot in K. Haroun thanked Mr Butt and said goodbye. 'But but but I will be here to escort you home,' he replied. 'Best seats will be kept; no question. Come when you're ready—I will be steady—then we'll go! Varoom! *No problem.*'

Haroun had been afraid that more Shouting Men would be waiting for Rashid here, but K was a remote place and

40

news of the storyteller's disastrous performance in the Town of G had not travelled as fast as Mr Butt's Mail Coach. So they were greeted by the Boss himself, the Top Man in the ruling party of the Valley, the Candidate in the forthcoming elections, on whose behalf Rashid had agreed to appear. This Boss was a fellow so shiny-faced and smooth, dressed in white bush-shirt and trousers so starchy-clean and neat, that the scruffy little moustache straggling over his upper lip seemed to have been borrowed from someone else: it was far too tawdry for a gent as slick as this.

The slick gent greeted Rashid with a movie-star smile whose insincerity made Haroun feel ill. 'Esteemed Mr Rashid,' he said. 'An honour for us. A legend comes to town.' If Rashid were to flop in the Valley of K the way he had in the Town of G, Haroun thought, this gent would soon change his tune. But Rashid looked pleased by the flattery, and anything that cheered him up was worth putting up with for the present . . . 'The name,' the slick gent said, inclining his head slightly and clicking his heels together, 'is Buttoo.'

'Almost the same as the Mail Coach driver!' Haroun exclaimed, and the slick gent with the ratty moustache threw up his hands in horror. 'Not *at all* the same as any bus driver,' he shrieked. 'Suffering Moses! Do you know to whom you speak? Do I *look* the bus-driver type?'

'Well, excuse *me*,' Haroun began, but Mr Buttoo was marching away, nose in air. 'Respected Mr Rashid, to the lakeside,' he commanded over his shoulder. 'Bearers will bring your bags.'

During the five-minute walk to the shore of the Dull Lake, Haroun began to feel distinctly uneasy. Mr Buttoo and his party (which now included Rashid and Haroun) were permanently surrounded by exactly one hundred and one heavily armed soldiers; and such ordinary people as Haroun noticed on the street wore extremely hostile expressions. 'There's a bad feeling in this town,' he told himself. If you live in a sad city you know unhappiness when you run into it. You can smell it on the night air, when the fumes of cars and trucks have faded away and the moon makes everything look clearer. Rashid had come to the Valley because he remembered it as the most joyful of places, but it was plain that trouble had found its way up here now.

'How popular can this Buttoo be if he needs all these soldiers to protect him?' Haroun wondered. He tried to whisper to Rashid that perhaps the slick gent with the face-fuzz wasn't the right fellow to support in the election campaign, but there were always too many soldiers within earshot. And then they reached the Lake.

Waiting for them was a boat in the shape of a swan. 'Nothing but the best for distinguished Mr Rashid,' crooned snooty Mr Buttoo. 'Tonight you stay in the finest houseboat on the Lake, as my guest. I trust it will not prove too humble for a grandee as exalted as you.' He sounded polite, but he was really being insulting, Haroun understood. Why did Rashid put up with it? Haroun climbed into the swan-boat, feeling irritated. Oarsmen in army uniform began to row.

Haroun looked down into the water of the Dull Lake. It

seemed to be full of strange currents, criss-crossing in intricate patterns. Then the swan-boat passed what looked like a carpet floating on the water's surface. 'Floating Garden,' Rashid told Haroun. 'You weave lotus-roots together to make the carpet and then you can grow vegetables right here on the Lake.' His voice had a melancholy ring again, so Haroun murmured, 'Don't be sad.'

'Sad? Unhappy?' yelped Snooty Buttoo. 'Surely eminent Mr Rashid is not dissatisfied with the arrangements?' Rashid the storyteller had always been incapable of inventing stories about himself, so he answered truthfully: 'Sir, not so. This is an affair of the heart.'

Why did you tell him that? Haroun thought fiercely, but Snooty Buttoo was delighted by the revelation. 'Not to worry, unique Mr Rashid,' he cried tactlessly. 'She may have left you *but there are plenty more fish in the sea.*'

'Fish?' Haroun thought, in a rage. 'Did he say fish?' Was his mother a pomfret? Must she now be compared to a glumfish or a shark? Really, Rashid should bop this Buttoo right on his stuck-up nose!

The storyteller trailed a hand listlessly in the waters of the Dull Lake. 'Ah, but you must go a long, long way to find an Angel Fish,' he sighed.

As if in response to his words, the weather changed. A hot wind began to blow, and a mist rushed at them across the water. The next thing they knew they could see nothing at all.

'Never mind the Angel Fish,' Haroun thought. 'I can't even, just at the moment, find the tip of my nose.'

3

The Dull Lake

Haroun had already smelled unhappiness on the night air, and this sudden mist positively stank of sadness and gloom. 'We should have stayed at home,' he thought. 'No shortage of long faces there.'

'Phoo!' shouted Rashid Khalifa's voice through the greeny-yellow mist. 'Who made *that* smell? Come on, admit.'

'It's the mist,' Haroun explained. 'It's a Mist of Misery.' But at once Snooty Buttoo's voice cried out, 'Lenient Mr Rashid, it seems the boy wants to cover up his stink-making with inventions. I fear he is too much like the folk of this foolish Valley—crazy for make-believe. What I must put up with! My enemies hire cheap fellows to stuff the people's ears with bad stories about me, and the ignorant people just lap it up like milk. For this reason I have turned, eloquent Mr Rashid, to you. You will tell happy stories, praising stories, and the people will believe you, and be happy, and vote for me.'

No sooner had Buttoo uttered these words than a harsh, hot wind blew across the Lake. The mist was dispersed, but now the wind burned into their faces, and the waters of the Lake became choppy and wild.

'It's not in the least Dull, this Lake,' exclaimed Haroun. 'In fact, it's positively Temperamental!' As the words left his lips, a penny dropped. 'This must be the Moody Land,' he burst out.

Now the Tale of the Moody Land was one of Rashid Khalifa's best-loved stories. It was the story of a magical country that changed constantly, according to the moods of its inhabitants. In the Moody Land, the sun would shine all night if there were enough joyful people around, and it would go on shining until the endless sunshine got on their nerves; then an irritable night would fall, a night full of mutterings and discontent, in which the air felt too thick to breathe. And when people got angry the ground would shake; and when people were muddled or uncertain about things the Moody Land got confused as well—the outlines of its buildings and lamp-posts and motor-cars got smudgy, like paintings whose colours had run, and at such times it could be difficult to make out where one thing ended and another began . . . 'Am I right?' Haroun asked his father. 'Is this the place the story was about?'

It made sense: Rashid was sad, so the Mist of Misery enveloped the swan-boat; and Snooty Buttoo was so full of hot air that it wasn't surprising he'd conjured up this boiling wind!

'The Moody Land was only a story, Haroun,' Rashid replied. 'Here we're somewhere real.' When Haroun heard his father say *only a story*, he understood that the Shah of Blah was very depressed indeed, because only deep despair could have made him say such a terrible thing.

Rashid, meanwhile, was arguing with Snooty Buttoo. 'Surely you don't want me to tell just sugar-and-spice tales?' he protested. 'Not all good stories are of that type. People can delight in the saddest of sob-stuff, as long as they find it beautiful.'

Snooty Buttoo flew into a rage. 'Nonsense, nonsense!' he shrieked. 'Terms of your engagement are crystal clear! For me you will please to provide up-beat sagas only. None of your gloompuss yarns! If you want pay, then just be gay.'

At once the hot wind began to blow with redoubled force; and as Rashid sank into silent wretchedness the greeny-yellow mist with the toilet stink came rushing towards them across the Lake; and the water was angrier than ever, slopping over the side of the swan-boat and rocking it alarmingly from side to side, as if it were responding to Buttoo's fury (and also, in point of fact, to Haroun's growing anger at Buttoo's behaviour).

The mist enfolded the swan-boat once again, and once again Haroun couldn't see a thing. What he heard were sounds of panic: the uniformed oarsmen crying out, 'O! O! Down we go!' and the infuriated shrieks of Snooty Buttoo, who seemed to take the weather conditions as a personal insult; and the more shrieks and yelps there were, the rougher the waters became, and the hotter and more violent the wind. Flashes of lightning and rolls of thunder lit up the mist, creating weird neon-like effects.

Haroun decided there was nothing for it but to put his Moody Land theory into practice. 'Okay,' he shouted into the mist. 'Everybody listen. This is very important: everybody, just stop talking. Not a word. Zip the Lips. Dead silence is very important, on the count of three, one, two, three.' A new note of authority had come into his voice, which surprised him as much as anyone, and as a result the oarsmen and Buttoo, too, obeyed him without a murmur. At once the boiling breeze fell away, the thunder and lightning stopped. Then Haroun made a conscious effort to control his irritation at Snooty Buttoo, and the waves calmed down the instant he cooled off. The smelly mist, however, remained.

'Just do one thing for me,' Haroun called to his father. 'Just this one thing. Think of the happiest times you can remember. Think of the view of the Valley of K we saw when we came through the Tunnel of I. Think about your wedding day. Please.'

A few moments later that malodorous mist tore apart like the shreds of an old shirt and drifted away on a cool night breeze. The moon shone down once more upon the waters of the Lake.

'You see,' Haroun told his father, 'it wasn't *only a story*, after all.'

Rashid actually laughed out loud in delight. 'You're a blinking good man in a tight spot, Haroun Khalifa,' he said with an emphatic nod. 'Hats off to you.'

'Gullible Mr Rashid,' cried Snooty Buttoo, 'surely you don't believe the lad's hocusing and pocusing? Freak weather conditions came, and then went. No more to be said.'

Haroun kept his feelings about Mr Buttoo to himself. He knew what he knew: that the real world was full of magic, so magical worlds could easily be real.

~ ~ ~

The houseboat was called *Arabian Nights Plus One*, because

50

(as Mr Buttoo boasted) 'even in all the Arabian Nights you will never have a night like this.' Each of its windows had been cut out in the shape of a fabulous bird, fish or beast: the Roc of Sindbad the Sailor, the Whale That Swallowed Men, a Fire-Breathing Dragon, and so on. Light blazed out through the windows, so that the fantastic monsters were visible from some distance, and seemed to be glowing in the dark.

Haroun followed Rashid and Mr Buttoo up a wooden ladder on to a verandah of intricately carved wood and into a living room with crystal chandeliers and throne-like seats with ornately brocaded cushions and walnut tables carved to look like flat-topped trees in which you could see tiny birds and also what looked like winged children but were, of course, fairies. The walls were lined with shelves full of leather-bound volumes, but most of these turned out to be fakes, concealing drinks cabinets and broom cupboards. One shelf, however, bore a set of real books written in a language Haroun could not read, and illustrated with the strangest pictures he had ever seen. 'Erudite Mr Rashid,' Buttoo was saying, 'you in your line of work will be interested in these. Here for your delectation and edification is the entire collection of tales known as *The Ocean of the Streams of Story*. If you ever run out of material you will find plenty in here.'

'Run out? What are you saying?' Rashid wildly asked, suddenly fearful that Buttoo had known, all along, about the terrible events in the Town of G. But Buttoo patted him on the shoulder: 'Touchy Mr Rashid! It was only a joke, a passing lightness, a cloud blown away by the breeze. Of course we await your recital with full confidence.'

But Rashid was down in the dumps again. It was time to call it a day.

The uniformed boatmen showed Rashid and Haroun to their bedrooms, which turned out to be even more opulent than the lounge. In the exact centre of Rashid's room stood an enormous painted wooden peacock. With little flourishes of the arms, the boatmen removed its back to reveal a large and comfortable bed. Haroun had the adjoining room, in which he found an equally outsize turtle, which likewise became a bed when the boatmen removed its shell. Haroun felt a little peculiar at the notion of sleeping on a turtle whose shell had been removed, but, remembering his manners, he said, 'Thank you, it is very pleasant.'

' "Very pleasant"?' hooted Snooty Buttoo from the doorway. 'Inappropriate young person, you are aboard *Arabian Nights Plus One*! "Very pleasant" does not cover it at all! Admit, at the very least, that it is all Super-Marvelloso, Incredibable, and wholly Fanta*stick*.'

Rashid gave Haroun a look that said 'We should have thrown this fellow into the Lake while we had the chance,' and interrupted Buttoo's screeches. 'It is, as Haroun has stated, very pleasant indeed. Now we will sleep. Goodnight.'

Buttoo stalked off to the swan-boat in a great huff. 'If people have no taste,' was his parting shot, 'the best things are a waste. Tomorrow, unappreciative Mr Rashid, it is your turn. Let us see how "very pleasant" your audience finds *you*.'

~ ~ ~

That night, Haroun found it difficult to get to sleep. He lay on the turtle's back in his favourite long nightshirt (bright red with purple patches) and tossed and turned, and just as he was about to drop off at long last he was woken up completely by noises from Rashid's room next door: a creaking and a rumbling and a groaning and a mumbling and then a low cry:

'It's no use—I won't be able to do it—I'm finished, finished for good!'

Haroun tiptoed to the connecting door and very carefully opened it, just a crack; and peeped. He saw the Shah of Blah in a plain blue nightshirt without any purple patches at all, pacing miserably around his peacock bed, muttering to himself while the floorboards creaked and moaned. ' "Only praising tales" indeed. I am the Ocean of Notions, not some office-boy for them to boss about! —But no, what am I saying? —I'll get up on stage and find nothing in my mouth but *arks*. —Then they'll slice me in pieces, it'll be all up with me, finito, *khattam-shud*! —Much better to stop fooling myself, give it all up, go into retirement, cancel my subscription. —Because the magic's gone, gone for ever, ever since she left.'

Then he turned to stare at the connecting door and called loudly, 'Who's there?' So there was nothing for it; Haroun had to say, 'It's me. I couldn't sleep. I think it's the turtle,' he added. 'It's just too weird.'

Rashid nodded gravely. 'It's a funny thing, but I've been

having trouble with this peacock, myself. For me a turtle would be better. How do you feel about the bird?'

'Definitely better,' Haroun admitted. 'A bird sounds okay.'

So Haroun and Rashid exchanged bedrooms; and that was why the Water Genie who visited *Arabian Nights Plus One* that night and crept into the Peacock Room found an unsleeping boy of about his own size staring him in the face.

~ ~ ~

To be precise: Haroun had just dozed off when he was woken by a creaking and a rumbling and a groaning and a mumbling; so his first thought was that his father hadn't found the turtle any easier to sleep on than the peacock. Then he realized that the noise wasn't coming from the Turtle Room, but from his own bathroom. The bathroom door was open and the light was on, and as Haroun watched he saw, silhouetted in the open doorway, a figure almost too astonishing for words.

It had an outsize onion for a head and outsize aubergines for legs, and it was holding a toolbox in one hand and what looked like a monkey wrench in the other. A burglar!

Haroun tiptoed towards the bathroom. The being inside was talking non-stop in a mumbling, grumbling way.

'Put it in, take it out. The fellow comes up here, so I have to come and install it, rush job, never mind my workload. —Then, wham, bam, he cancels his subscription, and guess who has to come back and take the equipment out, right away, pronto, you'd think there was a fire. —Now where did I put the blasted thing? —Has somebody been meddling? —Can't trust anybody any more. —Okay, okay, okay, let's be methodical. —Hot tap, cold tap, go halfway in between, go up in the air six inches, and there should be your Story Tap. —So where's it gone? Who's pinched it? —Whoops, what's this? —Oho, aha, is that where you are? Thought you could hide from me but I've got you now. Okay. Time to Disconnect.'

While this remarkable monologue was being delivered, Haroun Khalifa moved his head very, very slowly, until half an eye was looking around the door-jamb into the bathroom: where he saw a small, ancient-looking man, no bigger than himself, wearing a huge purple turban on his head (that was the 'onion') and baggy silk pajamas gathered at the ankles (those were the 'aubergines'). This little fellow sported an impressive full set of whiskers, of a most unusual colour: the palest, most delicate shade of sky blue.

Haroun had never seen blue hair before, and leant forward a little in curiosity; whereupon, to his horror, the floorboard on which he stood emitted a loud, unarguable creak. The blue-beard whirled about, spun all the way round three times, and disappeared; but in his haste he let the monkey wrench fall from his hand. Haroun dashed into the bathroom, grabbed it and held it close.

Slowly and in what seemed like a most disgruntled fashion (though it was hard for Haroun to be sure of this, as he'd never seen anyone materializing before), the little blue-beard reappeared in the bathroom. 'No kidding, enough's enough, party's over, fair's fair,' he snapped. 'Give it back.'

'No,' replied Haroun.

'The Disconnector,' the other pointed. 'Hand it over, return to sender, restore to rightful owner; give up, yield, surrender.'

Now Haroun noticed that the tool he held was no more like a monkey wrench than the blue-beard's head was like an onion: in other words, it had the general outline of a wrench, but it was somehow more fluid than solid, and was made up of thousands of little veins flowing with differently coloured liquids, all held together by some unbelievable, invisible force. It was beautiful.

'You're not getting it back,' Haroun said firmly, 'until you tell me what you're doing here. Are you a burglar? Shall I call the cops?'

'Mission impossible to divulge,' the little man sulked. 'Top secret, classified, eyes-only info; certainly not to be revealed to smarty-pants boys in red nightshirts with purple patches who snatch what isn't theirs and then accuse other people of being thieves.'

'Very well,' Haroun said. 'Then I'll wake my father.'

'No,' said the blue-beard sharply. 'No adults. Rules and regulations, totally forbidden, more than my job's worth. O, I knew this would be a terrible day.'

'I'm waiting,' said Haroun severely.

The little fellow drew himself up to his full height. 'I am the Water Genie, Iff,' he said crossly, 'from the Ocean of the Streams of Story.'

Haroun's heart thumped. 'Are you trying to claim you're really one of those Genies my father told me about?'

'Supplier of Story Water from the Great Story Sea,' the other bowed. 'Precisely; the same; none other; it is I. However, I regret to report, the gentleman no longer requires the service; has discontinued narrative activities, thrown in the towel, packed it in. He has cancelled his subscription. Hence my presence, for purposes of Disconnection. To which end, please to return my Tool.'

'Not so fast,' said Haroun, whose head was spinning, not only at the discovery that there really were Water Genies, that the Great Story Sea wasn't *only a story*, but also at the revelation that Rashid had quit, given up, buttoned his lip. 'I don't believe you,' he said to the Genie Iff. 'How did he send the message? I've been right with him almost all the time.'

'He sent it by the usual means,' Iff shrugged. 'A P2C2E.'

'And what is that?'

'Obvious,' said the Water Genie with a wicked grin. 'It's a Process Too Complicated To Explain.' Then he saw how upset Haroun was, and added: 'In this case, it involves Thought Beams. We tune in and listen to his thoughts. It's an advanced technology.'

'Advanced or not,' Haroun retorted, 'you've made a mistake this time, you're up the spout, you've got the wrong end of the stick.' He heard himself beginning to sound like the Water Genie, and shook his head to clear it. 'My father has definitely not given up. You can't cut off his Story Water supply.'

'Orders,' said Iff. 'All queries to be taken up with the Grand Comptroller.'

'Grand Comptroller of what?' Haroun wanted to know.

'Of the Processes Too Complicated To Explain, of course. At P2C2E House, Gup City, Kahani. All letters to be addressed to the Walrus.'

'Who's the Walrus?'

'You don't concentrate, do you?' Iff replied. 'At P2C2E House in Gup City there are many brilliant persons employed, but there is only one Grand Comptroller. They are the Eggheads. He is the Walrus. Got it now? Understood?'

Haroun absorbed all this information. 'And how does the letter get there?' he asked. The Water Genie giggled softly. 'It doesn't,' he answered. 'You see the beauty of the scheme.'

'I certainly don't,' Haroun retorted. 'And anyway, even if you do turn off your Story Water, my father will still be able to tell stories.'

'Anybody can tell stories,' Iff replied. 'Liars, and cheats, and crooks, for example. But for stories with that Extra Ingredient, ah, for those, even the best storytellers need the Story Waters. Storytelling needs fuel, just like a car; and if you don't have the Water, you just run out of Steam.'

'Why should I believe a word you say,' Haroun argued, 'when I can't see anything in this bathroom except for a perfectly ordinary bath, toilet, basin, and some perfectly ordinary taps marked Cold and Hot?'

'Feel here,' said the Water Genie, pointing to a patch of empty air six inches above the basin. 'Take the Disconnecting Tool, and just tap it against this space where you imagine nothing to be.' Dubiously, suspecting a trick, and only after instructing the Water Genie to stand well back, Haroun did as he was told. *Ding* went the Disconnecting Tool as it struck something extremely solid and extremely invisible.

'There she blows,' cried the Water Genie, grinning widely. 'The Story Tap: voilà.'

'I still don't get it,' Haroun frowned. 'Where *is* this Ocean of yours? And how does the Story Water get into this invisible Tap? How does the plumbing work?' He saw the wicked glint in Iff's eye and answered his own question with a sigh: 'Don't tell me, I know. By a Process Too Complicated To Explain.'

'Bull's-eye,' said the Water Genie. 'Got it in one, ten out of ten, spot on.'

Now Haroun Khalifa made a decision that would prove to be the most important decision of his life. 'Mr Iff,' he said politely but firmly, 'you must take me to Gup City to see the Walrus, so that I can get this stupid blunder about my father's Water supply reversed before it's too late.'

Iff shook his head and spread his arms wide. 'Impossible,' he said. 'No can do, it's off the menu, don't even dream about it. Access to Gup City in Kahani, by the shores of the Ocean of the Streams of Story, is strictly restricted, completely forbidden, one hundred per cent banned, except to accredited personnel; like, for instance, me. But you? No chance, not in a million years, no way, José.'

'In which case,' Haroun said sweetly, 'you'll just have to go back without this'—and here he waved the Disconnecting Tool in the blue-beard's face—'and see how

59

They like *that*.'

There was a long silence.

'Okay,' said the Water Genie. 'You've got me bang to rights, it's a done deal. Let's make tracks, scram, vamoose. I mean: if we're going, let's *go*.'

Haroun's heart sank rapidly towards his toes. 'You mean,' he stammered, '*now*?'

'Now,' said Iff. Haroun took a slow, deep breath.

'All right, then,' he said. 'Now.'

4

An Iff and a Butt

'So pick a bird,' the Water Genie commanded. 'Any bird.'

This was puzzling. 'The only bird around here is a wooden peacock,' Haroun pointed out, reasonably enough. Iff gave a snort of disgust. 'A person may choose what he cannot see,' he said, as if explaining something very obvious to a very foolish individual. 'A person may mention a bird's name even if the creature is not present and correct: crow, quail, hummingbird, bulbul, mynah, parrot, kite. A person may even select a flying creature of his own invention, for example winged horse, flying turtle, airborne whale, space serpent, aeromouse. To give a thing a name, a label, a handle; to rescue it from anonymity, to pluck it out of the Place of Namelessness, in short to identify it—well, that's a way of bringing the said thing into being. Or, in this case, the said bird or Imaginary Flying Organism.'

'That may be true where you come from,' Haroun argued. 'But in these parts stricter rules apply.'

'In these parts,' rejoined blue-bearded Iff, 'I am having my time wasted by a Disconnector Thief who will not trust in what he can't see. How much have you seen, eh, Thieflet? Africa, have you seen it? No? Then is it truly there? And submarines? Huh? Also hailstones, baseballs, pagodas? Gold-mines? Kangaroos, Mount Fujiyama, the North Pole? And the past, did it happen? And the future, will it come? Believe in your own eyes and you'll get into a lot of trouble, hot water, a mess.'

With that he plunged his hand into a pocket of his auberginey pajamas, and when he brought it forth again it was bunched into a fist. 'So take a look, or I should say a *gander*, at the enclosed.' He opened his hand; and Haroun's eyes almost fell out of his head.

Tiny birds were walking about on the Water Genie's palm; and pecking at it, and flapping their miniature wings to hover just above it. And as well as birds there were fabulous winged creatures out of legends: an Assyrian lion with the head of a bearded man and a pair of large hairy wings growing out of its flanks; and winged monkeys, flying saucers, tiny angels, levitating (and apparently air-breathing) fish. 'What's your pleasure, select, choose,' Iff urged. And although it seemed obvious to Haroun that these magical creatures were so small that they couldn't possibly have carried so much as a bitten-off fingernail, he decided not to argue and pointed at a tiny crested bird that was giving him a sidelong look through one highly intelligent eye.

'So it's the Hoopoe for us,' the Water Genie said, sounding almost impressed. 'Perhaps you know, Disconnector Thief, that in the old stories the Hoopoe is the bird that leads all other birds through many dangerous places to their ultimate goal. Well, well. Who knows, young Thieflet, who you may turn out to be. But no time for speculation now,' he concluded, and with that rushed to the window and hurled the tiny Hoopoe out into the night.

'What did you do that for?' hissed Haroun, not wishing to wake his father; at which Iff gave his wicked grin. 'A foolish notion,' he said innocently. 'A fancy, a passing whim. Certainly not because I know more about such matters than you, dear me, no.'

Haroun ran to the window, and saw the Hoopoe floating

on the Dull Lake, grown large, as large as a double bed, easily large enough for a Water Genie and a boy to ride upon its back.

'And off we go,' carolled Iff, much too loud for Haroun's liking; and then the Water Genie skipped up on to the window sill and thence to the Hoopoe's back—and Haroun, with scarcely a moment to reflect on the wisdom of what he was doing, and still wearing his long red nightshirt with the purple patches, and clutching the Disconnecting Tool firmly in his left hand, followed. As he settled down behind the Water Genie, the Hoopoe turned its head to inspect him with a critical but (Haroun hoped) friendly eye.

Then they took off and flew rapidly into the sky.

The force of their acceleration pushed Haroun deep into the comfortable, thick and somehow *hairy* feathers on the Hoopoe's back, feathers that seemed to gather around Haroun to protect him during the flight. He took a few moments to digest the large number of amazing things that had taken place in quick time.

Soon they were travelling so quickly that the Earth below them and the sky above both dissolved into a blur, which gave Haroun the feeling that they weren't moving at all, but simply floating in that impossible, blurry space. 'When the Mail Coach Driver, Butt, was rocketing up the Mountains of M, I had this same sense of floating,' he recalled. 'Come to think of it, this Hoopoe with its crest of feathers reminds me quite a bit of old Butt with his quiff of hair standing straight up on his head! —And if Butt's whiskers were somehow feathery, then this Hoopoe's feathers—as I noticed the moment we took off—have a distinctly hairy feel.'

Their speed increased again, and Haroun shouted into Iff's ear: 'No bird could fly so fast. Is this a machine?'

The Hoopoe fixed him with its glittering eye. 'You maybe have some objection to machines?' it inquired, in a loud, booming voice that was identical in every respect to the Mail Coach Driver's. And at once it went on: 'But but but you have entrusted your life to me. Then am I not worthy of a little of your respect? Machines also have their sense of self-esteem. —No need to gawp like that, young sir, I can't help it if I remind you of someone; at least, being a driver, he's a fellow who feels fond of a good, fast travel machine.'

'You can read my mind,' Haroun said, somewhat accusingly, because it wasn't entirely a pleasant feeling to have one's private ruminations bugged by a mechanical bird. 'But but but certainly,' answered the Hoopoe. 'Also I am communicating with you *telepathically*, because as you may observe I am not moving my beak, which must maintain its present configuration for aerodynamic reasons.'

'How are you doing that?' demanded Haroun, and back came the inevitable answer, quick as a flash of thought: 'By a P2C2E. A Process Too Complicated To Explain.'

'I give up,' said Haroun. 'Anyhow, do you have a name?'

'Whatever name you please,' replied the bird. 'Might I suggest, for obvious reasons, "Butt"?'

So it was that Haroun Khalifa the storyteller's son soared into the night sky on the back of Butt the Hoopoe with Iff the Water Genie as his guide. The sun rose; and after a time Haroun spotted something in the distance, a heavenly body like a large asteroid. 'That is Kahani, the Earth's second Moon,' said Butt the Hoopoe without moving its beak.

'But but but,' Haroun stammered (much to the Hoopoe's amusement), 'surely the Earth has just the one Moon? How could a second satellite have remained undiscovered for so long?'

'But but but it is because of Speed,' Butt the Hoopoe responded. 'Speed, most Necessary of Qualities! In any Emergency—fire, auto, marine—what is required above all things? Of course, Speed: of fire truck, ambulance, rescue ship. —And what do we prize in a brainy fellow? —Is it not his Quickness of Thought? —And in any sport, Speed (of foot, hand, eye) is of the Essence! —And what humans cannot do quickly enough, they build machines to do faster. —Speed, super Speed! If not for the Speed of Light, the universe would be dark and cold. —But if Speed brings light to reveal, it can also be used to conceal. The Moon, Kahani, travels so fast—wonder of wonders!—that no Earth instruments can detect it; also its orbit varies by one degree per circuit, so that in three hundred and sixty orbits it has overflown every spot upon the Earth. Variety of Behaviour assists in Evasion of Detection. But also, there are serious purposes for the variation of orbit: Story Water facilities must be provided across the entire planet with an even hand. Voom! Varoom! Only at High Speed may this be done. You appreciate the further bonuses of Machines?'

'Then is the Moon, Kahani, driven by mechanical means?'

Haroun asked, but Butt had turned its attention to practical matters. 'Moon approaching,' it said without moving its beak. 'Relative speed synchronized. Landing procedures initiated. Splashdown in thirty seconds, twenty-nine, twenty-eight.'

Rushing up towards them was a sparkling and seemingly infinite expanse of water. The surface of Kahani appeared—as far as Haroun's eye could see—to be entirely liquid. And what water it was! It shone with colours everywhere, colours in a brilliant riot, colours such as Haroun could never have imagined. And it was evidently a warm ocean; Haroun could see steam rising off it, steam that glowed in the sunlight. He caught his breath.

'The Ocean of the Streams of Story,' said Iff the Water Genie, his blue whiskers bristling with pride. 'Wasn't it worth travelling so far and fast to see?'

'Three,' said Butt the Hoopoe without moving its beak. 'Two, one, zero.'

~ ~ ~

Water, water everywhere; nor any trace of land . . . 'It's a trick,' cried Haroun. 'There's no Gup City here, unless I'm much mistaken. And no Gup City equals no P2C2E House, no Walrus, no point in being here at all.'

'Hold your horses,' said the Water Genie. 'Cool down, don't blow your top, keep your hair on. Explanations are in order, and are forthcoming, if you will only permit.'

'But this is the Middle of Nowhere,' Haroun went on. 'What do you expect me to do out here?'

'To be precise, this is the Deep North of Kahani,' the Water Genie replied. 'And what is available to us here is a short cut, avoidance of bureaucratic procedures, a means of cutting the red tape. Also, if I must truthfully admit, a means of solving our little difficulty without admitting to Guppee authorities my little mistake, my loss of Disconnecting Tool and subsequent blackmail by its Pincher. We are here in search of Wishwater.'

'Look for patches of the Ocean that shine with extra brightness,' Butt the Hoopoe added. 'That's Wishwater; use it properly and it can make your desires come true.'

'So persons in Gup need never be directly involved,' Iff went on. 'When your Wish is granted, you can return the Tool, and home you go to bed, and end of saga. Okay?'

'Oh, very well,' Haroun agreed somewhat doubtfully, and, it should be said, with a little regret, because he had been looking forward to seeing Gup City and learning more about the mysterious Processes Too Complicated To Explain.

'Tip-top type,' cried Iff in great relief. 'Good sport, prince among men, popular choice. —And hey presto! Wishwater ahoy!'

Butt paddled carefully towards the patch of brightness at which Iff was eagerly pointing, and came to a halt by its edge. The Wishwater gave off so dazzling a light that Haroun had to avert his gaze. —Now Iff the Water Genie reached inside his little gold-embroidered waistcoat and pulled out a small bottle made of many-faceted crystal, with a little golden cap. Swiftly unscrewing the cap, he drew the bottle through the bright water (whose glow was golden, too); and, fastening the lid once more, he passed the bottle carefully to Haroun. 'On your marks, be prepared, here goes,' he said. 'This is what you must do.'

This was the secret of the Wishwater: the harder you wished, the better it worked. 'So it's up to you,' Iff said. 'No fooling around, get down to it good and proper, do serious business, and the Wishwater will do serious business for you. And bingo! Your heart's desire will be as good as yours.'

Haroun sat astride Butt the Hoopoe and stared at the bottle in his hand. Just one sip, and he could regain for his father the lost Gift of the Gab! 'Down the hatch,' he cried courageously; unscrewed the cap; and took a goodly gulp.

Now the golden glow was all around him, and inside him, too; and everything was very, very still, as if the entire cosmos were waiting upon his commands. He began to focus his thoughts . . .

He couldn't do it. If he tried to concentrate on his father's lost storytelling powers and his cancelled Story Water subscription, then the image of his mother insisted on taking over, and he began to wish for her return instead, for everything to be as it had been before . . . and then his father's face returned, pleading with him, *just do this one thing for me, my boy, just this one little thing*; and then it was his mother again, and he didn't know what to think, what to wish—until with a jangling noise like the breaking of a thousand and one violin strings, the golden glow disappeared and he was back with Iff and the Hoopoe on the surface of the Sea of Stories.

'Eleven minutes,' said the Water Genie contemptuously.

'Just eleven minutes and his concentration goes, ka-bam, ka-blooey, ka-put.'

Haroun was filled with the shame of it, and hung his head.

'But but but this is disgraceful, Iff,' said Butt the Hoopoe without moving its beak. 'Wishes are not such easy things, as you know well. You, mister Water Genie, are upset because of your own error, because now we must go to Gup City after all, and there will be harsh words and hot water for you, and you are taking it out on the boy. Stop it! Stop it or I'll be annoyed.'

(Truly this was a most passionate, even excitable sort of machine, Haroun thought in spite of his unhappiness. Machines were supposed to be ultra-rational, but this bird could be genuinely temperamental.)

Iff looked at the red blush of humiliation that was all over Haroun's face and softened somewhat. 'Gup City it is,' he agreed. 'Unless, of course, you'd like to hand over the Disconnecting Tool and just call the whole thing off?'

Haroun shook his head, miserably.

'But but but you are still bullying the boy,' Butt the Hoopoe expostulated furiously without moving its beak. 'Change of plan, please, right away! Cheering-up procedures to be instituted at once. Give the lad a happy story to drink.'

'Not another drink,' said Haroun in a low, small voice. 'What are you going to make me fail at now?'

~ ~ ~

So Iff the Water Genie told Haroun about the Ocean of the Streams of Story, and even though he was full of a sense of

71

hopelessness and failure the magic of the Ocean began to have an effect on Haroun. He looked into the water and saw that it was made up of a thousand thousand thousand and one different currents, each one a different colour, weaving in and out of one another like a liquid tapestry of breathtaking complexity; and Iff explained that these were the Streams of Story, that each coloured strand represented and contained a single tale. Different parts of the Ocean contained different sorts of stories, and as all the stories that had ever been told and many that were still in the process of being invented could be found here, the Ocean of the Streams of Story was in fact the biggest library in the universe. And because the stories were held here in fluid form, they retained the ability to change, to become new versions of themselves, to join up with other stories and so become yet other stories; so that unlike a library of books, the Ocean of the Streams of Story was much more than a storeroom of yarns. It was not dead but alive.

'And if you are very, very careful, or very, very highly skilled, you can dip a cup into the Ocean,' Iff told Haroun, 'like so', and here he produced a little golden cup from another of his waistcoat pockets, 'and you can fill it with water from a single, pure Stream of Story, like so', as he did precisely that, 'and then you can offer it to a young fellow who's feeling blue, so that the magic of the story can restore his spirits. Go on now; knock it back, have a swig, do yourself a favour,' Iff concluded. 'Guaranteed to make you feel A-number-one.'

Haroun, without saying a word, took the golden cup and drank.

72

~ ~ ~

He found himself standing in a landscape that looked exactly like a giant chessboard. On every black square there was a monster: there were two-tongued snakes and lions with three rows of teeth, and four-headed dogs and five-headed demon kings and so on. He was, so to speak, looking out through the eyes of the young hero of the story. It was like being in the passenger seat of an automobile; all he had to do was watch, while the hero dispatched one monster after another and advanced up the chessboard towards the white stone tower at the end. At the top of the tower was (what else but) a single window, out of which there gazed (who else but) a captive princess. What Haroun was experiencing, though he didn't know it, was Princess Rescue Story Number S/1001/ZHT/420/41(r)xi; and because the princess in this particular story had recently had a haircut and therefore had no long tresses to let down (unlike the heroine of Princess Rescue Story G/1001/RIM/777/M(w)i, better known as 'Rapunzel'), Haroun as the hero was required to climb up the outside of the tower by clinging to the cracks between the stones with his bare hands and feet.

He was halfway up the tower when he noticed one of his hands beginning to change, becoming hairy, losing its human shape. Then his arms burst out of his shirt, and they too had grown hairy, and impossibly long, and had joints in

73

the wrong places. He looked down and saw the same thing happening to his legs. When new limbs began to push themselves out from his sides, he understood that he was somehow turning into a monster just like those he had been killing; and above him the princess caught at her throat and cried out in a faint voice:

'Eek, my dearest, you have into a large spider turned.'

As a spider he was able to make rapid progress to the top of the tower; but when he reached the window the princess produced a large kitchen knife and began to hack and saw at his limbs, crying rhythmically, '*Get* away spider, *go* back home'; and he felt his grip on the stones of the tower grow looser; and then she managed to chop right through the arm nearest her, and he fell.

~ ~ ~

'Wake up, snap out of it, let's have you,' he heard Iff anxiously calling. He opened his eyes to find himself lying full-length on the back of Butt the Hoopoe. Iff was sitting beside him, looking extremely worried and more than a little disappointed that Haroun had somehow managed to keep a firm grip on the Disconnecting Tool.

'What happened?' Iff asked. 'You saved the princess and walked off into the sunset as specified, I presume? But then why all this moaning and groaning and turning and churning? Don't you *like* Princess Rescue Stories?'

Haroun recounted what had happened to him in the story, and both Iff and Butt became very serious indeed. 'I can't believe it,' Iff finally said. 'It's a definite first, without parallel, never in all my born days.'

'I'm almost glad to hear it,' said Haroun. 'Because I was thinking, that wasn't the *most* brilliant way to cheer me up.'

'It's pollution,' said the Water Genie gravely. 'Don't you understand? Something, or somebody, has been putting filth into the Ocean. And obviously if filth gets into the stories, they go wrong. —Hoopoe, I've been away on my rounds too long. If there are traces of this pollution right up here in the Deep North, things at Gup City must be close to crisis. Quick, quick! Top speed ahead! This could mean war.'

'War with whom?' Haroun wanted to know.

Iff and Butt shivered with something very like fear.

'With the Land of Chup, on the Dark Side of Kahani,' Butt the Hoopoe answered without moving its beak. 'This looks like the doing of the leader of the Chupwalas, the Cultmaster of Bezaban.'

'And who's that?' Haroun persevered, beginning to wish he'd stayed in his peacock bed instead of getting muddled up with Water Genies and Disconnecting Tools and talking mechanical Hoopoes and story-oceans in the sky.

'His name,' whispered the Water Genie, and the sky darkened for an instant as he spoke it, 'is Khattam-Shud.'

Far away on the horizon, forked lightning glittered, once. Haroun felt his blood run cold.

5

About Guppees and Chupwalas

Haroun had not forgotten what his father had said about Khattam-Shud. 'Too many fancy notions are turning out to be true,' he thought. At once Butt the Hoopoe answered, without moving its beak: 'A strange sort of Story Moon our Kahani would be, if storybook things weren't everywhere to be found.' And Haroun had to admit that *that* was a reasonable remark.

They were speeding south to Gup City. The Hoopoe had chosen to remain on the water, zooming along like a speed-boat, spraying Story Streams in every direction. 'Doesn't it muddle up the stories?' Haroun inquired. 'All this turbulence. It must mix things up dreadfully.'

'No problem!' cried Butt the Hoopoe. 'Any story worth its salt can handle a little shaking up! Va-voom!'

Abandoning what was clearly not a profitable line of conversation, Haroun returned to more important matters. 'Tell me more about this Khattam-Shud,' he requested, and was utterly amazed when Iff replied in almost the very same words that Rashid Khalifa had used. 'He is the Arch-Enemy of all Stories, even of Language itself. He is the Prince of Silence and the Foe of Speech. At least', and here the Water Genie abandoned the somewhat too sonorous tone of the preceding sentences, 'that's what they say. When it comes to the Land of Chup and its people the Chupwalas, it's all mostly gossip and flim-flam, because it's generations since any of us went across the Twilight Strip into the Perpetual Night.'

'You'll have to forgive me,' Haroun broke in, 'but I'm going to need a little help with the geography.'

'Hmf,' sniffed Butt the Hoopoe. 'Poorly educated, I see.'

'That's totally illogical,' Haroun retorted. 'You're the one who's been boasting about how Speed has hidden this Moon from people on Earth. So it's unreasonable to expect us to know about its topographical features, principal exports and the like.'

But Butt's eye was twinkling. Really, there were major difficulties involved in talking to machines, Haroun thought. With their deadpan expressions, it was impossible to know when they were pulling your leg.

'Thanks to the genius of the Eggheads at P2C2E House,' Butt began, taking pity on Haroun, 'the rotation of Kahani has been brought under control. As a result the Land of Gup is bathed in Endless Sunshine, while over in Chup it's always the middle of the night. In between the two lies the Twilight Strip, in which, at the Grand Comptroller's command, Guppees long ago constructed an unbreakable (and also invisible) Wall of Force. Its goodname is Chattergy's Wall, named after our King, who of course had absolutely nothing to do with building it.'

'Hold on a minute,' Haroun frowned. 'If Kahani goes round the Earth, even if it goes *very* fast indeed, there must be moments when the Earth is between it and the sun. So it can't be true that one half is always in the daylight; you're telling stories again.'

'Naturally I'm telling stories,' Butt the Hoopoe replied. 'And if you have any arguments, please to take them up with the Walrus. Now excuse, please, while I pay attention ahead. Volume of traffic has dramatically increased.'

~ ~ ~

Haroun had plenty more questions to ask—why did the Chupwalas live in Permanent Night? Must it not be very cold indeed if the sun never shone at all? And what was Bezaban, or a Cultmaster, come to that?—but they were evidently nearing Gup City, because the waters around them and the skies above were filling up with mechanical birds every bit as fanciful as Butt the Hoopoe: birds with snake-heads and peacock-tails, flying fishes, dogbirds. And on the backs of the birds were Water Genies with whiskers of every possible hue, all wearing turbans and embroidered waistcoats and aubergine-shaped pajamas, and all looking so much like Iff that it was a good thing, in Haroun's opinion, that the colours of their whiskers were different enough to make it possible to tell them apart.

'Something most serious has occurred,' Iff commented. 'All units have been ordered back to base. Now if I had my Disconnecting Tool,' he added sharply, 'I would have received the order myself, because, as of course Thieflets do not know, there is a highly advanced transceiver built into the handle.'

'Luckily, however,' Haroun came back, just as sharply, 'since you half-poisoned me with that dirty story, you worked things out; so there's no harm done, except, perhaps, to me.'

Iff ignored this. And Haroun's attention was distracted as well, because he noticed that a large patch of what looked like a particularly thick and tough type of weed or vegetable of some sort was actually racing along right beside them, keeping pace with Butt the Hoopoe without apparent effort, while it waved vegetable-tentacles in the air in a most disturbing fashion. At the centre of the mobile vegetable patch was a single lilac flower with thick, fleshy leaves, of a type that Haroun had never seen before. 'What's *that*?' he inquired, pointing, even though he knew it was impolite to do so.

'A Floating Gardener, naturally,' said Butt the Hoopoe without moving its beak. That made no sense. 'You mean a Floating Garden,' Haroun corrected the bird, which gave a little snort. 'That's all *you* know,' it harrumphed. At that moment the high-speed vegetation actually reared up out of the water and proceeded to wind and knot itself around and about, until it had taken something like the shape of a man, with the lilac-coloured flower positioned in its 'head' where a mouth should be, and a cluster of weeds forming a rustic-looking hat. 'So it *is* a Floating Gardener after all,' Haroun realized.

The Floating Gardener was now running lightly over the surface of the water, showing no sign of sinking. 'How could he sink?' Butt the Hoopoe interjected. 'Would he not be a Sinking Gardener in that case? Whereas, as you observe, he floats; he runs, he walks, he hops. No problem.'

Iff called across to the Gardener, who at once nodded a brief greeting. 'Got a stranger with you. Very odd. Still. Your own business,' he said. His voice was as soft as flower petals (after all, he was actually speaking through those lilac lips), but his manner was somewhat abrupt. 'I thought all you Guppees were chatterboxes,' Haroun whispered to Iff. 'But this Gardener doesn't say much.'

'He *is* talkative,' Iff rejoined. 'For a Gardener, anyhow.'

'How do you do,' Haroun called across to the Gardener, thinking that, as he was the stranger, it was his business to introduce himself. 'Who are you?' the Gardener asked in his soft but abrupt way, without breaking his stride. Haroun told him his name and the Gardener gave another curt nod.

'Mali,' he said. 'Floating Gardener First Class.'

'Please,' Haroun said in his nicest voice, 'what does a Floating Gardener do?'

'Maintenance,' answered Mali. 'Untwisting twisted Story Streams. Also unlooping same. Weeding. In short: Gardening.'

'Think of the Ocean as a head of hair,' said Butt the Hoopoe, helpfully. 'Imagine it's as full of Story Streams as a thick mane is full of soft, flowing strands. The longer and thicker a head of hair, the knottier and more tangled it gets. Floating Gardeners, you can say, are like the hairdressers of the Sea of Stories. Brush, clean, wash, condition. So now you know.'

Iff asked Mali, 'What's this pollution? When did it start? How bad is it?'

Mali answered the questions in sequence. 'Lethal. But nature as yet unknown. Started only recently, but spread is very rapid. How bad? Very bad. Certain types of story may take years to clean up.'

'For example?' Haroun piped up.

'Certain popular romances have become just long lists of shopping expeditions. Children's stories also. For instance, there is an outbreak of talking helicopter anecdotes.'

With that, Mali fell silent, and the rush to Gup City continued. A few minutes later, however, Haroun heard more new voices. They were like choruses, many voices at a time speaking in perfect unison, and they were full of froth and bubbles. Finally Haroun worked out that they were actually coming up from beneath the surface of the Ocean. He looked down into the waters and saw two fearsome sea-monsters right beside the racing Hoopoe, swimming so close to the surface that they were almost surfing on the spray thrown up by Butt as it sped along.

From their roughly triangular shape and their iridescent colouring, Haroun deduced that they were Angel Fish of some variety, though they were as big as giant sharks and had literally dozens of mouths, all over their bodies. These mouths were constantly at work, sucking in Story Streams and blowing them out again, pausing only to speak. When they did so, Haroun noted, each mouth spoke with its own voice, but all the mouths on each individual fish spoke perfectly synchronized words.

'Hurry! Hurry! Don't be late!' bubbled the first fish.

'Ocean's ailing! Cure can't wait!' the second went on.

Butt the Hoopoe was once again kind enough to enlighten Haroun. 'These are Plentimaw Fishes,' it said. 'They acquire their goodname from the fact that you have no doubt registered, viz., that they have plenty of maws, i.e., mouths.'

'So,' thought Haroun, filled with wonder, 'there really are Plentimaw Fish in the Sea, just as old Snooty Buttoo said; and I *have* travelled a long way, just as my father said, and

I've learned that a Plentimaw Fish can be an Angel Fish as well.'

'Plentimaw Fishes always go in two's,' Butt added without moving its beak. 'They are faithful to partners for life. To express this perfect union they speak, only and always, in rhyme.'

These particular Plentimaw Fishes seemed unhealthy to Haroun. Their multiple mouths frequently spluttered and coughed, and their eyes looked inflamed and pink. 'I'm no expert,' Haroun called to them, 'but are you both quite well?'

The replies came swiftly, punctuated by bubbling coughs:

'All this bad taste! Too much dirt!'

'Swimming in the Ocean starts to hurt!'

'Call me Bagha! This is Goopy!'

'Excuse our rudeness! We feel droopy!'

'Eyes feel rheumy! Throat feels sore!'

'When we're better, we'll talk more.'

'As you correctly guessed, all Guppees love to talk,' Iff said in an aside. 'Silence is often considered rude. Hence the Plentimaws' apology.' —'They seem to be talking okay to me,' Haroun replied. —'Normally, each mouth says something different,' Iff explained. 'That makes plenty more talk. For them, this is like silence.'

'Whereas for a Floating Gardener a few short sentences are called talkativeness,' Haroun sighed. 'I don't think I'll ever get the hang of this place. What do the fish do, anyway?'

Iff replied that the Plentimaw Fishes were what he called 'hunger artists'—'Because when they are hungry they swallow stories through every mouth, and in their innards miracles occur; a little bit of one story joins on to an idea from another, and hey presto, when they spew the stories out they are not old tales but new ones. Nothing comes from nothing, Thieflet; no story comes from nowhere; new stories are born from old—it is the new combinations that make them new. So you see, our artistic Plentimaw Fishes really create new stories in their digestive systems—so just think how sick they must be feeling now! All these filthied-up sagas passing through their insides, front to back, top to bottom, side to side—no wonder they look green about the gills!'

The Plentimaws surfaced to utter one more wheezy couplet:

'Things are worse than we've ever known!'

'And the worst place is down in our Old Zone.'

On hearing this, the Water Genie clapped his hand to his forehead, almost dislodging his turban. 'What? What?' Haroun insisted on knowing; and so a now-even-more-preoccupied Iff grudgingly explained that the Old Zone in the southern polar region of Kahani was an area to which hardly anybody went any more. There was little demand for the ancient stories flowing there. 'You know how people are, new things, always new. The old tales, nobody cares.' So the Old Zone had fallen into disuse; but it was believed that all the Streams of Story had originated long ago in one of the currents flowing north across the Ocean from the Wellspring, or Source of Stories, that was located, according to legend, near the Moon's South Pole.

86

'And if the Source itself is poisoned, what will happen to the Ocean—to us all?' Iff almost wailed. 'We have ignored it for too long, and now we pay the price.'

'Hold on to hats,' Butt the Hoopoe interrupted. 'Hitting the brake now. Gup City dead ahead. Record time! Va-va-va-voom! *No problem.*'

'It's amazing what you can get accustomed to, and at what speed,' Haroun reflected. 'This new world, these new friends: I've just arrived, and already none of it seems very strange at all.'

~ ~ ~

Gup City was all excitement and activity. Waterways criss-crossed the city in all directions—for the capital of the Land of Gup was built upon an Archipelago of one thousand and one small islands just off the Mainland—and at present these waterways thronged with craft of every shape and size, all packed with Guppee citizens, who were similarly diverse, and who all wore worried expressions on their faces. Butt the Hoopoe, with Mali on one side and Goopy and Bagha on the other, advanced (more slowly now) through this floating crowd, heading, like everyone else, for the Lagoon.

The Lagoon, a beautiful expanse of multicoloured waters, stood between the Archipelago, where most Guppees made their homes in intricately carved wooden buildings with roofs of corrugated silver and gold, and the Mainland, where a gigantic formal garden came down in terraces right to the water's edge. In this Pleasure Garden were fountains and pleasure-domes and ancient spreading trees, and around it were the three most important buildings in Gup, which looked like a trio of gigantic and elaborately iced cakes: the Palace of King Chattergy, with its grand balcony overlooking the Garden; to its right the Parliament of Gup, known as the *Chatterbox* because debates there could run on for weeks or months or even, occasionally, years, on account of the Guppee fondness for conversation; and to its left, the towering edifice of P2C2E House, a huge building from which whirrs and clanks were constantly heard, and inside which were concealed one thousand and one Machines Too Complicated To Describe, which controlled the Processes Too Complicated To Explain.

Butt the Hoopoe brought Iff and Haroun to the steps at the water's edge. The boy and the Water Genie disembarked and joined the throng gathering in the Pleasure Garden, while those Guppees who preferred the water (Floating Gardeners, Plentimaw Fishes, mechanical birds) remained in the Lagoon. In the Pleasure Garden, Haroun noticed large numbers of Guppees of an extraordinary thinness, dressed in entirely rectangular garments covered in writing. 'Those,' Iff told him, 'are the famous Pages of Gup; that is to say, the army. Ordinary armies are made up of platoons and regiments and suchlike; our Pages are organized into Chapters and Volumes. Each Volume is headed by a Front, or Title, Page; and up there is the leader of the entire "Library", which is our name for the army—General Kitab himself.'

'Up there' was the balcony of the Palace of Gup, on which the city's dignitaries were now assembling. It was easy to identify General Kitab, a weatherbeaten old gent with a rectangular uniform made of finely-tooled gold-inlay leather, of the sort Haroun had sometimes seen on the covers of old and valuable books. Then there was the Speaker (that is, the leader) of the Chatterbox, a plump fellow who was even now talking unstoppably to his colleagues on the balcony; and a frail, small white-haired gentleman wearing a circlet of gold and a tragic look. This was presumably King Chattergy himself. The last two figures on the balcony were harder for Haroun to identify. There was a young and at present extremely worked-up fellow with a dashing but somehow foolish look to him ('Prince Bolo, the fiancé of King Chattergy's only child, his daughter the Princess Batcheat,' Iff whispered to Haroun); and lastly, a person with a hairless head of quite spectacular smoothness and shininess, bearing on his upper lip a disappointingly insignificant moustache that looked like a piece of a dead mouse. 'He reminds me of Snooty Buttoo,' Haroun whispered to Iff. 'Never mind—nobody you know. But who is this fellow?'

In spite of whispering, he was overheard by many of the people now crowding together in the full Pleasure Garden. They turned in disbelief to inspect this stranger whose ignorance was so remarkable (and whose nightshirt was equally unusual), and Haroun noticed that among the crowd were many men and women who, like the man on the balcony, had smooth, shiny and hairless heads. These people all wore the white coats of laboratory technicians and were, clearly, the Eggheads of P2C2E House, the geniuses who operated the Machines Too Complicated To Describe (or M2C2Ds) which made possible the Processes Too Complicated To Explain.

'Are you—?' he began, and they interrupted him, for being Eggheads, they were extremely quick on the uptake.

'We are the Eggheads,' they nodded, and then, with looks on their faces that said *we can't believe you don't know this*, they pointed at the shiny fellow on the grand balcony and said, 'He is the Walrus.'

'*He's* the Walrus?' Haroun burst out, astounded. 'But he's nothing like a walrus! Why do you call him that?'

'It's on account of his thick, luxuriant walrus moustache,' one of the Eggheads replied, and another added admiringly, 'Look at it! Isn't it the *best*? So *hairy*. So silky-smooth.'

'But . . . ' Haroun began, and then stopped when Iff dug him hard in the ribs. 'I suppose if you're as hairless as these Eggheads,' he told himself, 'even that pathetic dead mouse on the Walrus's upper lip looks like the greatest thing you've ever seen.'

King Chattergy raised his hand; the crowd fell silent. (An unusual event in Gup City.)

The King attempted to speak, but words failed him, and shaking his head unhappily he stepped back. It was Prince Bolo who burst into impetuous speech. 'They have seized her,' he cried in his dashing, foolish voice. 'My Batcheat, my Princess. The servants of the Cultmaster purloined her some hours back. Churls, dastards, varlets, hounds! By gum, they will pay for this.'

General Kitab took up the story. 'A blasted business, confound it! Her whereabouts are not known, but most probably she will be kept prisoner in the Citadel of Chup, the Ice Castle of Khattam-Shud in Chup City, at the heart of the Perpetual Night. Spots and fogs! A bad business. Harrumph.'

'We have sent messages to Cultmaster Khattam-Shud,' continued the Speaker of the Chatterbox. 'These messages concerned both the vile poison being injected into the Ocean of the Streams of Story, and the abduction of Princess Batcheat. We demanded that he put a stop to the pollution and also return, within seven hours, the kidnapped Lady. Neither demand has been met. I have to inform you, therefore, that a state of war now exists between the Lands of Gup and Chup.'

'Extreme urgency is of the essence,' the Walrus told the crowd. 'The poisons that are spreading so rapidly will destroy the entire Ocean if steps are not taken to get to the bottom of the problem.'

'Save the Ocean!' cried the crowd.

'Save Batcheat!' shouted Prince Bolo. This confused the crowd for a few moments; then, good-naturedly, they altered their cry:

'For Batcheat and the Ocean!' they exclaimed, and Prince Bolo looked satisfied enough with that.

Iff the Water Genie put on his most winning expression. 'Well, now it's war, young Thieflet,' he said with mock-regret. 'That means nobody at P2C2E House will have any time for your little request. You may as well hand back that Disconnecting Tool; then, what do you say, I'll have you taken home for nothing, completely free! There—what could be fairer than that?'

Haroun clutched the Disconnector with all his might and stuck out his lower lip mutinously. 'No Walrus, no Disconnector,' he said. 'And that's flat.'

Iff appeared to accept this philosophically. 'Have a chocolate,' he said, and produced from one of his many waistcoat pockets a jumbo-sized version of Haroun's favourite chocolate bar. Realizing that he was starving hungry, Haroun gratefully accepted. 'I didn't know you made these here on Kahani,' he said.

'We don't,' Iff replied. 'Food production on Kahani is strictly basic. For tasty and wicked luxury items we have to go to Earth.'

'So this is where the Unidentified Flying Objects come from,' Haroun marvelled. 'And that's what they've been after: snacks.'

Just then there was a small commotion on the palace balcony. Prince Bolo and General Kitab went inside for a moment, then returned to announce that Guppee patrols who had entered the outlying areas of the Twilight Strip, looking for clues to the whereabouts of the Princess Batcheat, had arrested a stranger—a highly suspicious person who could give no satisfactory account of himself or explain what he was doing in the Strip. 'I will question this spy before you all, myself!' shouted Bolo, and though General Kitab looked a little embarrassed by that idea, he did not argue. Now a quartet of Pages led a man on to the balcony, a man wearing a long blue nightshirt with his hands tied behind his back and a sack over his head.

When the sack was removed, Haroun's mouth fell open and the unfinished chocolate bar fell from his hand.

The man standing and shivering on the palace balcony between Prince Bolo and General Kitab was Haroun's father, Rashid Khalifa the storyteller, the unhappy Shah of Blah.

6

The Spy's Story

he capture of the Earthling 'spy' created a buzz of horror
in the Pleasure Garden; and when he identified himself
as 'just a storyteller, and a long-time subscriber to your
own Story Water service', the general outrage only
grew. Haroun started to force his way somewhat rudely
through the crowd. Many eyes stared suspiciously at this
second Earthling, also wearing a nightshirt, who was
pushing and shoving and appeared to be in quite a state. Up
the seven terraces of the Pleasure Garden went Haroun,
heading for the palace balcony; and on his way he heard
many Guppees muttering: 'Our own subscriber! —How
could he betray and help the Chupwalas? —That poor
Princess Batcheat—what did she ever do, except sing so
badly it almost split our eardrums?—and she's no oil
painting, either, but that's no excuse—you can't trust these
Earthlings, that's the truth.' Haroun, getting angrier by the
minute, pushed even harder through the crowd. At his heels
came Iff, the Water Genie, crying: 'Wait on, patience is a
virtue, where's the fire?' But Haroun would not be stopped.

'What do Guppees do to spies, anyhow?' he yelled bad-
temperedly at Iff. 'I suppose you rip out their fingernails one
by one until they confess. Do you kill them slowly and
painfully, or quickly with a million volts in an electric
chair?' The Water Genie (and every other Guppee who
heard this outburst) looked horrified and affronted. 'Where
did you pick up such bloodthirstiness?' Iff cried. 'Absurd, an
outrage, I never heard the like.' —'Well, then, what?'
Haroun insisted. —'I don't know,' panted Iff as he struggled
to keep up with the charging boy. 'We've never caught a

spy before. Maybe we should scold him. Or make him stand in the corner. Or write *I must not spy* one thousand and one times. Or is that too severe?'

Haroun did not answer, because they had finally arrived under the palace balcony. Instead, he shouted at the top of his voice: 'Dad! What are *you* doing here?'

Every single Guppee stared at him in amazement, and Rashid Khalifa (who was still shivering with cold) looked no less surprised. 'Oh, goodness,' he said, shaking his head. 'Young Haroun. You surely are the most unexpected of boys.'

'He's not a spy,' Haroun shouted. 'He's my father, and the only thing wrong with him is that he's lost the Gift of the Gab.'

'That's right,' said Rashid gloomily through chattering teeth. 'Go on, tell everyone, broadcast it to the whole world.'

~ ~ ~

Prince Bolo sent one of his Pages to escort Haroun and Iff to the royal quarters in the heart of the palace. This Page, who didn't look much older than Haroun, introduced himself as 'Blabbermouth', which, as it turned out, was a popular name in Gup for girls as well as boys. Blabbermouth was wearing one of the Pages' regulation rectangular tunics on which Haroun observed the text of a story called 'Bolo and the Golden Fleece'. 'That's strange,' he said to himself. 'I thought that story was about someone else.'

As they made their way through the mazy passages of the royal palace of Gup, Haroun noted that many other Pages of the Royal Guard were dressed in half-familiar stories. One Page wore the tale of 'Bolo and the Wonderful Lamp'; another, 'Bolo and the Forty Thieves'. Then there was 'Bolo the Sailor', 'Bolo and Juliet', 'Bolo in Wonderland'. It was all very puzzling, but when Haroun asked Blabbermouth about the stories on the uniforms, the Page only replied, 'This is *not* the time for a discussion of *fashion points*. The Dignitaries of Gup are *waiting* to question your father and you.' It seemed to Haroun, however, that his question had embarrassed Blabbermouth, whose face had reddened noticeably. 'Well, all in good time,' Haroun told himself.

In the Throne Room of the palace, Rashid the storyteller was telling his story to Prince Bolo, General Kitab, the Speaker and the Walrus. (King Chattergy had retired, feeling unwell owing to too much worrying about Batcheat.) He was wrapped in a blanket and had his feet in a bowl of steaming hot water. 'How I arrived in Gup, you will be wondering,' he began, sipping a bowl of soup. 'It is through certain dietary procedures.'

Haroun looked disbelieving, but the others were listening intently. 'As a frequent insomnia sufferer,' Rashid went on, 'I have learnt that particular foodstuffs, properly prepared, will (a) induce sleep, but also (b) carry the sleeper wherever he may wish. It is a process known as Rapture. And with sufficient skill, a person may choose to wake up in the place to which the dream takes him; to wake up, that is to say, *inside the dream.* I wished to travel to Gup; but owing to a slight directional miscalculation, I woke up in the Twilight Strip, dressed only in this inappropriate garb; and I froze, I confess it freely, I froze half to death.'

'What are these foodstuffs?' the Walrus asked in a very interested voice. Rashid had recovered sufficiently to make his mysterious-eyebrow face and reply, 'Ah, but you must permit me my little secrets. Let us say, moonberries, comet's tails, planet rings, washed down with a little primal soup. This soup, by the way, is very fine,' he concluded on a different note.

'If they believe that story, they'll believe anything,' Haroun thought. 'Now surely they'll lose their tempers and give him the Third Degree.' What actually happened was that Prince Bolo gave a loud, dashing, foolish laugh and thumped Rashid Khalifa on the back, making him blow soup out of his mouth. 'A wit as well as an adventurer,' he said. 'Good show! Fellow, I like you well.' And with that he slapped his thigh.

'What credulous souls these Guppees are,' Haroun mused. 'And gentle, too. Iff could have fought me for his Disconnecting Tool, but he made no attempt to get it, not even when I was out cold. And if they would sentence a real spy to no more than a thousand and one lines, then they are peaceful people indeed. But if they have to fight a war, what then? They'll be completely hopeless, a lost cause . . . ' And here his thoughts tailed off, because he had been on the verge of adding, *'Khattam-shud.'*

'In the Twilight Strip,' Rashid Khalifa was saying, 'I have

seen bad things, and heard worse. There is an encampment
there, of the Chupwala Army. Such black tents, wrapped in
such a fanatical silence! —Because it's true what you have
heard rumours of: the Land of Chup has fallen under the
power of the "Mystery of Bezaban", a Cult of Dumbness or
Muteness, whose followers swear vows of lifelong silence
to show their devotion. Yes; as I moved stealthily among
the Chupwalas' tents I learnt this. In the old days the
Cultmaster, Khattam-Shud, preached hatred only towards
stories and fancies and dreams; but now he has become
more severe, and opposes Speech for any reason at all. In
Chup City the schools and law-courts and theatres are all
closed now, unable to operate because of the Silence Laws.
—And I heard it said that some wild devotees of the
Mystery work themselves up into great frenzies and sew
their lips together with stout twine; so they die slowly of
hunger and thirst, sacrificing themselves for the love of
Bezaban . . . '

'But who or what is Bezaban?' Haroun burst out. 'You
may all know, but I don't have a clue.'

'Bezaban is a gigantic idol,' Rashid told his son. 'It is a
colossus carved out of black ice, and stands at the heart of
Khattam-Shud's fortress-palace, the Citadel of Chup. They
say the idol has no tongue, but grins frightfully, showing its
teeth, which are the size of houses.'

'I think I wish I hadn't asked that,' said Haroun.

'Chupwala soldiers were flitting around in that murky
Twilight,' Rashid resumed his story. 'They wore long cloaks
through whose swirlings I sometimes caught sight of a cruel,

dully glinting dagger blade.

'But, sirs, you all know the stories about Chup! —That it is a place of shadows, of books that wear padlocks and tongues torn out; of secret conspiracies and poison rings. —Why should I wait near that awful camp? With bare feet, blue with cold, I went towards the distant light on the horizon. As I walked, I came to Chattergy's Wall, the Wall of Force; and, sirs, it is in bad repair. There are many holes, and movement through it is easily achieved. The Chupwalas know this already—I saw them across the Wall—I witnessed the kidnapping of Batcheat with my own eyes!'

'What's that you say?' shouted Bolo, leaping to his feet and striking a dashing and slightly foolish pose. 'Why have you waited so long to tell us? Zounds! Proceed; for pity's sake, proceed.' (When Bolo spoke like this, the other Dignitaries all looked vaguely embarrassed and averted their eyes.)

'I was struggling through the tangles of thorn-bushes towards the Ocean's rim,' Rashid continued, 'when a swan-boat of silver and gold approached. In it was a young woman with long, long hair, wearing a circlet of gold, and singing, please excuse, the ugliest sounding song I have ever heard. In addition, her teeth, her nose . . . '

'You needn't go on,' the Speaker of the Chatterbox interrupted. 'That was Batcheat all right.'

'Batcheat, Batcheat!' lamented Bolo. 'Shall I never hear your sweet sweet voice, or gaze upon your delicate face again?'

'What was she doing there?' the Walrus demanded.

'Those are dangerous parts.'

Here Iff, the Water Genie, cleared his throat. 'Sirs,' he said, 'maybe you don't know it but the young people of Gup do go into the Twilight Strip just occasionally, that is to say sometimes, that is to say most frequently. Living in the sunlight all the time, they wish to see the stars, the Earth, the Other Moon shining in the sky. It is a daredevil thing to do. And always there was, they thought, Chattergy's Wall to protect them. Dark, my sirs, has its fascinations: mystery, strangeness, romance . . .'

'Romance?' Prince Bolo cried, drawing his sword. 'Foul Water Genie! Shall I run you through? You dare to suggest that my Batcheat went there . . . for love?'

'No, no,' Iff cried in panic. 'A thousand apologies, I take it back, no offence.'

'No need to worry on that score,' Rashid quickly reassured Prince Bolo, who slowly, slowly, replaced his sword in its scabbard. 'She was with her handmaidens and no one else. They were giggling about Chattergy's Wall, about wanting to go up to it and touch it. "I want to know what it's like, this famous and invisible thing," I heard her say. "If the eye can't see it, maybe the finger can feel, maybe the tongue can taste." Just then a Chupwala party, which, unknown to Batcheat or myself, had been watching the Princess from the thorn-bushes, having plainly come through a hole in the Wall, seized the ladies and carried them off, kicking and shrieking, towards the tents of Chup.'

'And what kind of man are you,' sneered Prince Bolo rudely, 'that you stayed hidden and did nothing to save them from such a fate?'

The Walrus, the Speaker and the General looked pained at this latest remark of the Prince's, and Haroun got red in the face with rage. 'That Prince—how dare he,' he whispered fiercely to Iff. 'If it weren't for that sword, I'd . . . I'd . . . '

'I know,' the Water Genie whispered back. 'Princes can get like that. But don't worry. We don't really let him do anything important around here.'

'What would you have preferred?' Rashid answered Bolo with great dignity. 'That I, unarmed, dressed in a nightshirt and half-dead with cold, should have leapt like a romantic fool from my hiding-place, and got myself captured or killed? Then who would have brought you the news—who would be able, now, to show you the way to the Chupwala encampment? You be a hero if you wish, Prince Bolo; some people prefer good sense to heroism.'

'You should apologize, Bolo,' the Speaker murmured and, with much swaggering and scowling, the Prince finally did so. 'I was too sharp,' he said. 'Truly, we are grateful for your news.'

'There's one thing more,' Rashid said. 'As the Chupwala soldiers hauled the Princess away, I heard them say a terrible thing.'

'What thing?' Bolo shouted, leaping about. 'If they insulted her . . .'

' "The Great Feast of Bezaban is coming soon," one of them said,' answered Rashid. ' "Why not, on the day, offer our Idol this Guppee Princess as a sacrifice? We'll stitch up her lips, and rename her the Dumb Princess—the Princess

Khamosh." Then they laughed.'

A hush fell over the Throne Room. And of course it was Bolo who spoke first. 'Now there is not a second to lose! Assemble the armed forces—all the Pages, every Chapter, every Volume! —To war, to war! For Batcheat, only Batcheat!'

'For Batcheat and the Ocean,' the Walrus reminded him.

'Yes, yes,' Prince Bolo huffily said. 'The Ocean also; naturally, of course, very well.'

'If you wish,' Rashid the storyteller said, 'I will lead you to the Chupwala tents.'

'Good man,' Bolo shouted, thumping him on the back again. 'I did you wrong; you're a champion.'

'If you're going,' Haroun said to his father, 'don't think you can leave me behind.'

~ ~ ~

Although the Endless Daylight of Gup gave Haroun the strange feeling that time was standing still, he realized he was exhausted. He found that he could not resist the slow drooping of his eyelids; and then his body was possessed by so magnificent a yawn that it attracted the attention of everyone in that august Throne Room. Rashid Khalifa asked if Haroun might be given a bed for the night; and so, in spite of his protestations ('I'm not in the *least* sleepy—really, I'm *not*'), Haroun was packed off for the night. The Page, Blabbermouth, was told to lead him to his room.

Blabbermouth led Haroun along corridors, up staircases, down staircases, along more corridors, through doorways, around corners, into courtyards, out of courtyards, on to balconies, and down corridors again. While they walked, the Page (who seemed not to be able to contain the words a moment longer) unleashed an anti-Batcheat tirade. 'Fool of a girl,' Blabbermouth said. 'Now if *my* fiancée got herself kidnapped because she was crazy enough to go into the Twilight Strip just to go *gooey* over *stars* in the *sky* and, even worse, to *touch* the stupid *Wall*, for goodness' sake, then don't imagine *I'd* start a war to get her back; I'd say good riddance, especially with her *nose*, her *teeth*, but no need to go into all that, and I haven't even *mentioned* her *singing*, you wouldn't believe how horrible, and instead of letting her *rot* we're all going to go in after her and probably get ourselves *killed* because we won't be able to see properly in the *dark* . . . '

'Are we getting to my bedroom soon?' Haroun inquired. 'Because I'm not sure how much more of this I can take.'

'And these *uniforms*, you wanted to know about the *uniforms*,' Blabbermouth continued, ignoring him, and continuing briskly on through halls, down spiral stairways, and along passageways. 'Well, *whose* idea do you think *those* were? *Hers*, obviously, *Batcheat's*, and she decided to "take the wardrobe of the Pages of the Royal Household in *hand*" to make us into walking *love letters*, that was her first idea, and after an eternity of having to wear *kissy-poo* and *cuddly-bunny* and *vomitous* texts like that she changed her mind and had all the greatest stories in the *world* rewritten as if her Bolo was the hero or something. So now instead of Aladdin and Ali Baba and Sindbad it's Bolo, Bolo, Bolo, can you *imagine*, people in Gup City *laugh* at us to our *faces*, to say *nothing* of behind our *backs*.'

Then, with a triumphant grin, Blabbermouth stopped outside an extremely imposing doorway and announced, 'Your bedroom'; at which the doors burst open, and guards seized both of them by the ears and told them to be on their way before they were thrown into the deepest dungeon in the palace, because they had arrived at the bedchamber of King Chattergy himself.

'We're lost, aren't we?' Haroun said.

'So it's a *complicated* palace and we're a *little* lost,' Blabbermouth admitted. 'But aren't we having a nice *chat*?'

This remark so exasperated Haroun that in his exhaustion he swung an arm loosely at Blabbermouth's head, catching the Page by surprise and knocking off the maroon velvet cap on his head . . . on *her* head, that is to say, because as the cap fell to the ground a great torrent of shiny black hair cascaded down over Blabbermouth's shoulders. 'What did you do *that* for?' wailed the Page. 'Now you've spoilt *everything*.'

'You're a girl,' Haroun said, a little obviously.

'*Shhh*,' hissed Blabbermouth, stuffing her hair back under her cap. 'You want to get me the *sack* or *what*?' She dragged Haroun into a little alcove and drew a curtain to screen them from view. 'You think it's *easy* for a girl to get a job like this? Don't you know girls have to *fool people* every *day* of their *lives* if they want to get *anywhere*? You probably had your whole *life* handed to you on a *plate*, probably got a whole *mouth* full of *silver spoons*, but some of us have to *fight*.'

'You mean that just because you're a girl you aren't

allowed to be a Page?' Haroun asked, sleepily.

'I suppose *you* only do what you're *told*,' Blabbermouth hotly rejoined. 'I suppose *you* always eat up all the *food* on your *plate*, even the *cauliflower*. I suppose you . . . '

'At least I could do something perfectly simple like showing someone where their bedroom is,' Haroun butted in. Blabbermouth suddenly gave a broad, wicked grin. 'I suppose *you* always go to bed when you're told to,' she said. 'And you wouldn't be at *all* interested in going up on to the palace *roof* through this secret passageway right *here*.'

And so, after Blabbermouth had pushed the button hidden in an elaborately carved wooden panel on one of the alcove's curved walls, and after they had climbed the staircase that came into view when the panel slid away, Haroun sat on the flat roof of the palace in what was of course still dazzling sunshine, and gazed out at the view of the Land of Gup, and of the Pleasure Garden in which preparations for war were being made, and of the Lagoon in which a great flotilla of mechanical birds was assembling, and out across the endangered Ocean of the Streams of Story. Haroun realized, quite suddenly, that he had never felt more completely alive in his life, even if he was ready to drop with fatigue. And at that exact moment, without a word, Blabbermouth took three soft balls made of golden silk from one of her pockets, tossed them in the air so that they caught the sunlight, and began to juggle.

She juggled behind her back, over and under her leg, with her eyes closed, and lying down, until Haroun was speechless with admiration; and every so often she'd throw all the balls high into the air, reach into her pockets, and produce more of the soft golden spheres, until she was juggling nine balls, then ten, then eleven. And every time Haroun thought, 'She can't possibly keep them all up', she'd add even more balls to her whirling galaxy of soft, silken suns.

It occurred to Haroun that Blabbermouth's juggling reminded him of the greatest performances given by his father, Rashid Khalifa, the Shah of Blah. 'I always thought storytelling was like juggling,' he finally found the voice to say. 'You keep a lot of different tales in the air, and juggle them up and down, and if you're good you don't drop any. So maybe juggling is a kind of storytelling, too.'

Blabbermouth shrugged, caught up all her golden balls, and tucked them away in her pockets. 'I don't know anything about *that*,' she said. 'I just wanted you to *know* who you were *dealing* with here.'

~ ~ ~

Haroun woke up many hours later in a darkened room (they had finally found his bedroom, after asking another Page for help, and he had fallen asleep five seconds after Blabbermouth drew the heavy curtains and said goodnight).

Someone was sitting on his chest; someone's hands were around his throat, squeezing it tightly.

It was Blabbermouth. 'Rise and shine,' she whispered menacingly. 'And if you tell *anyone* about me, then the *next* time you're asleep I *won't stop squeezing*; you may be a *good* boy but I can be a *very* bad girl *indeed.*'

'I won't tell, I promise,' Haroun gasped, and Blabbermouth released her grip, and grinned. 'You're okay, Haroun Khalifa,' she said. 'Now get out of bed before I have to drag you out. Time to report for duty. There's an army in the Pleasure Garden, getting ready to march.'

7

Into the Twilight Strip

'Here's another Princess Rescue Story I'm getting mixed up in,' thought Haroun, yawning sleepily. 'I wonder if this one will go wrong, too.' He didn't have to wonder for long. 'By the way,' Blabbermouth said casually. 'I took the little *liberty*, at a certain Water Genie's *express request*, of removing, from under your pillow, the Disconnecting Tool which you *stole* without so much as a *by-your-leave*.'

Haroun, aghast, searched frantically through his bed-clothes; but the Disconnector was gone, and with it the means of getting an interview with the Walrus in order to get Rashid's Story Water subscription renewed . . . 'I thought you were my friend,' he said accusingly. Blabbermouth shrugged. 'Your plan's *totally* out of *date*, anyway,' she replied. 'Iff told me all about it; but your *father's* here *himself* now, *he* can sort out his *own* problem.'

'You don't get it,' Haroun sadly said. 'I wanted to do it for him.'

There was a fanfare of trumpets from the Pleasure Garden. Haroun jumped out of bed and ran to the window. Down below him in the Garden was a great commotion, or *rustling*, of Pages. Hundreds upon hundreds of extremely thin persons in rectangular uniforms that did, in fact, rustle exactly like paper (only much more loudly) were rushing about the Garden in a most disorderly fashion, arguing about the precise order in which they should line up, crying, '*I'm* before you!' —'Don't be ridiculous, that wouldn't make sense, it's plain that *I* must stand ahead of you . . . '

All the Pages were numbered, Haroun noted, so it should

have been a simple matter to decide upon their sequence. He put this to Blabbermouth, who answered, 'Things aren't quite as *simple* as that in the *real world*, mister. There are *plenty* of Pages with the *same numbers*; so they have to work out which '*Chapter*' they belong in, in which '*Volume*', and so forth. Also quite often there are *errors* in the uniforms, so they've got on *completely* the *wrong* number anyway.'

Haroun watched the Pages jostling and arguing and shaking their fists in the air and tripping each other up, just to be awkward, and remarked: 'It doesn't seem like a very disciplined army to me.'

'You shouldn't judge a *book* by its *cover*,' snapped Blabbermouth, after which (evidently a little put out) she announced she couldn't wait for Haroun any longer, as she was already late; and of course Haroun had to race after her, still in his red nightshirt with the purple patches, without even brushing his teeth or hair, and without having had time to point out a number of flaws in her arguments. As they ran along corridors, up staircases, down staircases, through galleries, into courtyards, out of courtyards, along yet more corridors, Haroun panted, 'In the first place, I wasn't "judging the book by the cover", as you suggested, because I could see all the *Pages*—and, in the second place, this isn't the "real world", not at all.'

'Oh, *isn't* it?' Blabbermouth shot back. 'That's the *trouble* with you *sad city* types: you think a place has to be *miserable* and *dull as ditchwater* before you believe it's real.'

'Would you do me a favour?' Haroun panted. 'Would you ask somebody the way?'

~ ~ ~

By the time they reached the Garden, the Guppee Army—or 'Library'—had completed the process of 'Pagination and Collation'—that is to say, arranging itself in an orderly fashion—which Haroun had observed from his bedroom window. 'See you *later*,' gasped Blabbermouth, and fled in the direction of the Royal Pages in their maroon velvet caps who were standing neatly beside Prince Bolo as he capered and pranced dashingly (but a little foolishly) on his mechanical flying horse.

Haroun spotted Rashid without difficulty. His father had evidently overslept, too, and was, like Haroun, still tousle-headed and wearing nothing but a somewhat crumpled and dirty blue nightshirt.

Standing with Rashid Khalifa in a small pavilion full of playing fountains—and now waving cheerfully at Haroun, with the Disconnecting Tool in his hand—was the blue-bearded Water Genie, Iff.

Haroun put on a burst of speed, and reached them only just in time. ' . . . a great honour to meet you,' Iff was saying. 'Especially as it is no longer required to call you the Father of a Little Thief.' Rashid frowned in puzzlement as Haroun arrived and said hurriedly, 'I'll explain later,' and gave Iff a glare that reduced even him to silence. To change the subject, Haroun added, 'Dad, wouldn't you like to meet my *other* new friends—the really interesting ones, I mean?'

~ ~ ~

'For Batcheat and the Ocean!'

The Guppee forces were ready to depart. The Pages had climbed into the long Barge-Birds waiting for them in the Lagoon; Floating Gardeners and Plentimaw Fishes were likewise at the ready; Water Genies astride their various flying machines stroked their whiskers impatiently. Rashid Khalifa climbed aboard Butt the Hoopoe behind Iff and Haroun. Mali, Goopy and Bagha were by their side. Haroun introduced them to his father; then, with a great cry, they were off.

'How stupid we were not to dress more sensibly!' Rashid lamented. 'In these nightshirts, we'll freeze solid in a few hours.'

'Fortunately,' said the Water Genie, 'I brought along a supply of Laminations. Say please and thank you nicely and I might let you have some.'

'Please and thank you nicely,' Haroun said quickly.

Laminations turned out to be thin, transparent garments as shiny as dragonfly wings. Haroun and Rashid pulled long shirts of this material over their nightshirts, and drew on long leggings, too. To their amazement the Laminations stuck so tightly to their nightshirts and legs that they seemed to have vanished altogether. All Haroun could make out was a faint gleamy sheen on his clothes and skin that hadn't been there before.

'You won't feel the cold now,' Iff promised.

They had left the Lagoon, and Gup City was diminishing

behind them; Butt the Hoopoe kept pace with the other speeding mechanical birds, and sprays of water were all around. 'How life does change,' Haroun marvelled. 'Only last week, I was a boy who had never seen snow in my entire life, and now here I am, heading into an ice-wilderness on which the sun never shines, wearing nothing but my nightclothes and with some strange transparent stuff as my only protection from the cold. It's a case of out of the frying pan into the fire.'

'Ridiculous,' said Butt the Hoopoe, having read Haroun's mind. 'A case of out of the fridge into the freezer, you mean.'

'That's unbelievable,' cried Rashid Khalifa. 'It spoke without moving its beak.'

~ ~ ~

The Guppee armada was well under way. Gradually Haroun became aware of what started out as a low buzz of noise and grew to a dull murmur and finally a rumbling roar. It took him a while to recognize that this was the sound of Guppees engaged in non-stop conversation and debate of growing intensity. 'Sound carries over water,' he remembered, but this quantity of sound would have carried even over a dry and barren waste. Water Genies, Floating Gardeners, Plentimaw Fishes and Pages were loudly arguing out the pro's and con's of the strategy to which they were committed.

Goopy and Bagha were as vocal on the subject as any

of the other Plentimaws, and their bubbling cries of dissatisfaction grew louder as they moved further and further towards the Twilight Strip and the Land of Chup beyond:

'Saving Batcheat! What a notion!'

'What matters is to save the Ocean!'

'That's the plan to set in motion—'

'—Find the source of the Poison Potion!'

'The Ocean's the important thing—'

'—Worth more than the daughter of any king.'

Haroun was rather shocked. 'That sounds like mutinous talk to me,' he suggested, and Iff, Goopy, Bagha and Mali found that very interesting indeed. 'What's a Mutinus?' asked Iff, curiously. 'Is it a plant?' Mali inquired.

'You don't understand,' Haroun tried to say. 'It's an Adjective.'

'Nonsense,' said the Water Genie. 'Adjectives can't talk.'

'Money talks, they say,' Haroun found himself arguing (all this argument around him was proving infectious), 'so why not Adjectives? Come to that, why not anything?'

The others fell silent for a sullen moment, and then simply changed the subject back to the issue of the day: which should take priority, saving Batcheat or the Ocean? But Rashid Khalifa gave Haroun a wink, which made him feel a little less crushed.

The sounds of heated quarrelling came across the water from the Barge-Birds: 'I say it's a Wild Goose Chase to go after Batcheat!' —'Yes, and what's more, she looks like a Wild Goose, too.' —'How dare you, sirrah? That's our beloved Princess you're talking about; our estimable Prince

Bolo's intended and beauteous bride!' —'Beauteous? Have you forgotten that voice, that nose, those teeth . . . ?' —'Okay, okay. No need to go into that.' Haroun noticed that old General Kitab himself, mounted on a winged mechanical horse very like Bolo's, was flitting from Barge-Bird to Barge-Bird to keep in touch with the various discussions; and such was the freedom evidently allowed to the Pages and other citizens of Gup, that the old General seemed perfectly happy to listen to these tirades of insults and insubordination without batting an eyelid. In fact, it looked to Haroun as if the General was on many occasions actually provoking such disputes, and then joining in with enthusiastic glee, sometimes taking one side, and at other times (just for fun) expressing the opposite point of view.

'What an army!' Haroun mused. 'If any soldiers behaved like this on Earth, they'd be court-martialled quick as thinking.'

'But but but what is the point of giving persons Freedom of Speech,' declaimed Butt the Hoopoe, 'if you then say they must not utilize same? And is not the Power of Speech the greatest Power of all? Then surely it must be exercised to the full?'

'It's certainly getting a lot of exercise today,' Haroun replied. 'I don't believe you Guppees could keep a secret to save your lives.'

'We could *tell* secrets to save our lives, however,' Iff replied. 'I, for example, know a large many secrets of great juiciness and interest.'

'I, also,' Butt the Hoopoe said without moving its beak.

'Shall we begin?'

'No,' said Haroun flatly. 'We shall not begin.' Rashid was beside himself with delight. 'Well, well, well, young Haroun Khalifa,' he chortled, 'you certainly did make some blinking funny friends.'

And so the Guppee armada proceeded on its merry way, with all its members busily dissecting General Kitab's most secret battle-plans (which, of course, he cheerfully revealed to anyone who cared to ask). These plans were itemized, scrutinized, rationalized, analysed, mulled over, chewed over, made much of, made little of, and even, after interminable wranglings, agreed. And when Rashid Khalifa, who was beginning to be as dubious as Haroun about the value of so much loose talk, ventured to question its wisdom,—then Iff and Butt and Mali and Goopy and Bagha fell to arguing about this question, too, with as much energy and passion as before.

Only Prince Bolo remained aloof. Prince Bolo rode his flying mechanical steed through the sky at the head of the Guppee forces, saying nothing, looking neither to left nor right, his eyes fixed on the far horizon. For him there was no argument; Batcheat came first; the issue was beyond dispute.

'How is it,' Haroun wondered, 'that Bolo can be so certain, when every other Guppee in this armada seems to take for ever to make up his mind about anything?'

It was Mali, the Floating Gardener, striding along beside him, walking on the water, who replied in flowery voice through fleshy lilac lips.

'It is Love,' Mali said. 'It is all for Love. Which is a wonderful and dashing matter. But which can also be a very foolish thing.'

~ ~ ~

The light failed slowly, then more quickly. They were in the Twilight Strip!

Looking into the distance, where darkness gathered like a storm-cloud, Haroun felt his courage weaken. 'With our absurd armada,' he despaired, 'how can we ever succeed in that world, where there isn't even light to see the enemy by?' The closer they came to the shores of the Land of Chup, the more formidable the prospect of the Chupwala Army became. It was a suicidal mission, Haroun became convinced; they would be defeated, and Batcheat would perish, and the Ocean would be irreparably ruined, and all stories would come to a final end. The sky was dim and purplish now, and it echoed his fatalistic mood.

'But but but don't take this seriously,' Butt the Hoopoe intervened kindly. 'You are suffering from a Heart-Shadow. It happens to most people the first time they see the Twilight Strip and the Darkness beyond. I, of course, do not suffer in this way, having no Heart: a further advantage, by the way, of being a machine. —But but but don't worry. You'll get acclimatized. It will pass.'

'To look on the bright side,' said Rashid Khalifa, 'these Laminations certainly work. I can't feel the cold at all.'

~ ~ ~

Goopy and Bagha were coughing and spluttering more and more. The coastline of Chup was in sight, and a bleak-looking thing it was; and in these coastal waters the Ocean of the Streams of Story was in the filthiest state Haroun had seen up to now. The poisons had had the effect of muting the colours of the Story Streams, dulling them all down towards greyness; and it was in the colours that the best parts of the Stories in those Streams were encoded: their vividness, lightness and vivacity. So the loss of colour was a terrible kind of damage. Worse yet, the Ocean in these parts had lost much of its warmth. No longer did the waters give off that soft, subtle steam that could fill a person with fantastic dreams; here they were cool to the touch and clammy to boot.

The poison was cooling the Ocean down.

Goopy and Bagha panicked:

'If this all goes on (hic, cough) we're all lost!'

'The Ocean will (cough, hic) become a Frost!'

Then it was time to set foot on the shores of Chup.

On those twilit shores, no bird sang. No wind blew. No voice spoke. Feet falling on shingle made no sound, as if the pebbles were coated in some unknown muffling material. The air smelt stale and stenchy. Thorn-bushes clustered around white-barked, leafless trees, trees like sallow ghosts. The many shadows seemed to be alive. Yet the Guppees were not attacked as they landed: no skirmishes on the shingle. No archers hiding in the bushes. All was stillness and cold. The silence and darkness seemed content to bide their time.

'The further into the darkness they lure us, the more the odds are in their favour,' said Rashid in a dull voice. 'And they know we will come, because they are holding Batcheat.'

'I thought Love was supposed to conquer all,' Haroun thought, 'but on this occasion it looks as if it could make monkeys—or mincemeat—of the lot of us.'

A beachhead was established, and tents had been raised to make the first Guppee camp. General Kitab and Prince Bolo sent Blabbermouth to fetch Rashid Khalifa. Haroun, delighted to see the Page again, went along with his father. 'Storyteller,' cried Bolo in his most swashbuckling manner, 'now is the hour when you must lead us to the Chupwala tents. Great matters are afoot! Batcheat's release cannot be delayed!'

Haroun and Blabbermouth, along with the General, the Prince, and the Shah of Blah, went stealthily through the thorn-bushes, to scout out the neighbourhood; and after a short time Rashid stopped and pointed, without saying a word.

There was a small clearing up ahead, and in this leafless glade was a man who looked almost like a shadow, and who held a sword whose blade was dark as night. The man was alone, but turned and leapt and kicked and slashed his sword constantly, as though battling an invisible opponent. Then, as they drew nearer, Haroun saw that the man was actually fighting *against his own shadow*; which, in turn, was fighting back with equal ferocity, attention and skill.

'Look,' whispered Haroun, 'the shadow's movements don't match the man's.' Rashid silenced him with a glance, but what he had said was the truth: the shadow plainly possessed a will of its own. It dodged and ducked, it stretched itself out until it was as long as a shadow cast by the last rays of the setting sun, and then it bunched itself as tight as a shade at noon, when the sun is directly overhead. Its sword lengthened and shrank, its body twisted and altered constantly. How could one ever hope to defeat such an opponent, wondered Haroun.

The shadow was attached to the warrior at the feet, but other than that seemed to be entirely free. It was as though its life in a land of darkness, of being a shadow concealed in shadows, had given it powers undreamt of by the shadows of a conventionally lit world. It was an awesome sight.

The warrior was a striking figure, too. His long, sleek hair hung to his waist in a thick ponytail. His face was painted green, with scarlet lips, exaggerated black brows and eyes, and white stripes on his cheeks. His bulky battle-dress of leather guards and thick thigh- and shoulder-pads made him seem even larger than he truly was. And his athleticism and swordsmanship were beyond anything Haroun had ever seen. No matter what tricks his shadow played, the warrior was its equal. And as they fought each other, standing toe to toe, Haroun began to think of their combat as a dance of great beauty and grace, a dance danced in perfect silence, because the music was playing inside the dancers' heads.

Then he glimpsed the warrior's eyes, and a chill struck at

his heart. What terrifying eyes they were! Instead of whites, they had *blacks*; and the irises were grey as twilight, and the pupils were white as milk. 'No wonder the Chupwalas like the dark,' Haroun understood. 'They must be blind as bats in the sunlight, because their eyes are the wrong way round, like a film negative that somebody forgot to print.'

As he watched the Shadow Warrior's martial dance, Haroun thought about this strange adventure in which he had become involved. 'How many opposites are at war in this battle between Gup and Chup!' he marvelled. 'Gup is bright and Chup is dark. Gup is warm and Chup is freezing cold. Gup is all chattering and noise, whereas Chup is silent as a shadow. Guppees love the Ocean, Chupwalas try to poison it. Guppees love Stories, and Speech; Chupwalas, it seems, hate these things just as strongly.' It was a war between Love (of the Ocean, or the Princess) and Death (which was what Cultmaster Khattam-Shud had in mind for the Ocean, and for the Princess, too).

'But it's not as simple as that,' he told himself, because the dance of the Shadow Warrior showed him that silence had its own grace and beauty (just as speech could be graceless and ugly); and that Action could be as noble as Words; and that creatures of darkness could be as lovely as the children of the light. 'If Guppees and Chupwalas didn't hate each other so,' he thought, 'they might actually find each other pretty interesting. Opposites attract, as they say.'

Just at that moment the Shadow Warrior stiffened; turned his strange eyes upon the bush behind which the Guppee party was hiding; and then sent his Shadow stretching out towards them. It reared up over them, holding its immensely elongated sword. The Shadow Warrior (sheathing *his* sword, which had no effect on the Shadow) walked slowly over to their hiding place. His hands were moving furiously in something like a dance of rage or hate. Faster and faster, more and more emphatic grew his hand movements; and then, in what might have been disgust, he let his hands drop, and began (horror of horrors!) to speak.

8

Shadow Warriors

The effort of producing sounds twisted the Shadow
Warrior's already-striking face (green skin, scarlet lips,
white-striped cheeks, etc.) into dreadful, contorted
shapes. 'Gogogol,' he gurgled. 'Kafkafka,' he coughed.

'Eh? What's that? What's the fellow saying?' demanded
Prince Bolo loudly. 'Can't make out a single word.'

'What a *poser*, I *swear*,' Blabbermouth hissed at Haroun.
'Our Bolo. Talking so *big* and *rude* because he thinks it'll
stop us from noticing that he's *scared* out of his *pants*.'

Haroun wondered why Blabbermouth remained in Prince
Bolo's service when she had such a low opinion of the
gentleman; but he kept his mouth shut, partly because he
didn't want her to say something cutting and scornful to
him; partly because he had started to like her a good deal,
which made any opinion of hers okay with him; but mostly
because there was a giant Shadow with a huge sword
looming over them, and a Warrior grunting and spitting at
them from a few feet away, and in short this was no time for
chit-chat.

'If, as it is said, people in the Land of Chup hardly talk at
all these days, because of the Cultmaster's decrees, then it's
not surprising that this Warrior has temporarily lost control
of his voice,' Rashid Khalifa was explaining to Prince Bolo,
who was unimpressed.

'It's too bad,' he said. 'Really, why people can't speak
properly, it beats me.'

The Shadow Warrior, ignoring the Prince, made further
rapid hand gestures at Rashid, and managed to croak out a
few words. 'Murder,' it said. 'Spock Obi New Year.'

'So it's murder he plans,' cried Bolo, putting his hand upon the hilt of his sword. 'Well, he won't have it all his own way, I promise him *that*.'

'Bolo,' said General Kitab, 'Dash it all, will you be quiet? Spots and fogs! This Warrior is trying to tell us something.'

The Shadow Warrior's hand movements became agitated and a little desperate: he twiddled his fingers into different positions, held his hands at different angles, pointed at different parts of his body, and repeated, hoarsely: 'Murder. Murder. Spock Obi New Year.'

Rashid Khalifa smacked his forehead. 'I've got it,' he exclaimed. 'What a fool I am. He's been talking to us fluently all the time.'

'Don't be ridiculous,' Prince Bolo put in. 'You call those grunts *fluency*?'

'It's the hand movements,' Rashid answered, showing considerable restraint at Bolo's burblings. 'He has been using the Language of Gesture. As for what he said, it wasn't "murder", but *Mudra*. That's his name. He's been trying to introduce himself! *Mudra. Speak Abhinaya.* That's what he's been saying. "Abhinaya" is the name of the most ancient Gesture Language of all, which it just so happens I know.'

Mudra and his Shadow instantly began nodding furiously. Now the Shadow sheathed its sword, too, and began to use Gesture Language as rapidly as Mudra himself, so that Rashid was obliged to plead, 'Hang on. One at a time, please. And slowly; I haven't done this for a long time, and you're going too fast for me.'

After a few moments of 'listening' to the hands of Mudra

and his Shadow, Rashid turned to General Kitab and Prince Bolo with a smile. 'Nothing to worry about,' he said. 'Mudra is a friend. Also, this is a lucky meeting—for we have here none other than the Champion Warrior of Chup, considered by most Chupwalas to be second in authority only to Cultmaster Khattam-Shud himself.'

'If he's Khattam-Shud's number two man,' Prince Bolo exclaimed, 'then we really are in luck. Let's seize him and put him in chains and tell the Cultmaster we'll only release him if we get Batcheat back safe and sound.'

'And how do you propose to capture him?' General Kitab mildly asked. 'I do not think he wishes to be captured, you know. Harrumph.'

'Please listen,' Rashid urged. 'Mudra is no longer an ally of the Cultmaster's. He has become disgusted with the growing cruelty and fanaticism of the Cult of the tongueless ice-idol Bezaban, and has broken off relations with Khattam-Shud. He came here, to this twilit wilderness, to think out what he should do next. If you wish, I can interpret his Abhinaya for you.'

General Kitab nodded, and Mudra began to 'speak'. Haroun noticed that the Language of Gesture involved more than just the hands. The position of the feet was important, too, and eye movements as well. In addition, Mudra possessed a phenomenal degree of control over each and every muscle in his green-painted face. He could make bits of his face twitch and ripple in the most remarkable way; and this, too, was a part of his 'speaking', his Abhinaya.

'Don't think all Chupwalas follow Khattam-Shud or

worship his Bezaban,' Mudra *said* in his silent, dancing way (and Rashid translated his 'words' into ordinary speech). 'Mostly they are simply terrified of the Cultmaster's great powers of sorcery. But if he were defeated, most people in Chup would turn to me; and though my Shadow and I are warriors, we are both in favour of Peace.'

Now it was the Shadow's turn to 'speak'. 'You must understand that in the Land of Chup, Shadows are considered the equals of the people to whom they are joined,' it began (with Rashid translating again). 'Chupwalas live in the dark, you know, and in the dark a Shadow doesn't have to be one single shape all the time. Some Shadows—such as my goodself—learn how to change ourselves, simply by wishing to do so. Imagine the advantages! If a Shadow doesn't care for the clothes sense or hairstyle of the person to whom it's attached, it can simply choose a style for itself! A Chupwala's Shadow can be graceful as a dancer even if its owner is clumsy as an oaf. You comprehend? What's more: in the Land of Chup, a Shadow very often has a stronger personality than the Person, or Self, or Substance to whom or to which it is joined! So often the Shadow leads, and it is the Person or Self or Substance that follows. And of course there can be quarrels between the Shadow and the Substance or Self or Person; they can pull in opposite directions—how often have I witnessed that!—but just as often there is a true partnership, and mutual respect. —So Peace with the Chupwalas means Peace with their Shadows, too. —And among the Shadows, also, Cultmaster Khattam-Shud has made terrible trouble.'

Mudra the Shadow Warrior resumed the narrative. Quicker and quicker moved his hands; and his facial muscles rippled and twitched in a most excited way; and his legs danced nimbly and fast. Rashid had to work very hard to keep up with him. 'Khattam-Shud's black magic has had fearsome results,' Mudra revealed. 'He has plunged so deeply into the Dark Art of sorcery that he has become Shadowy himself—changeable, dark, more like a Shadow than a Person. And as he has become more Shadowy, so his Shadow has come to be more like a Person. And the point has come at which it's no longer possible to tell which is Khattam-Shud's Shadow and which his substantial Self—because he has done what no other Chupwala has ever dreamt of—that is, he has separated himself from his Shadow! He goes about in the darkness, entirely Shadowless, and his Shadow goes wherever it wishes. *The Cultmaster Khattam-Shud can be in two places at once!*'

At this point Blabbermouth, who had been gazing at the Shadow Warrior with something very like adoration or devotion, burst out, 'But that's the *worst news* in the *world*! It was going to be almost *impossible* to defeat him *once*—and now you tell us we'll have to beat him *twice*?'

'Precisely so,' said the grim gestures of Mudra's Shadow. 'Furthermore, this new, doubled Khattam-Shud, this man-shadow and shadow-man, has had a very harmful effect on the friendships between Chupwalas and their Shadows. Now many Shadows are resentful of being joined to Chupwalas at the feet; and there are many quarrels.'

'It is a sad time,' Mudra's gestures concluded, 'when a Chupwala cannot even trust his own Shadow.'

A silence fell, as General Kitab and Prince Bolo mulled over everything that Mudra and his Shadow had 'said'. Then Prince Bolo burst out, 'Why should we believe this creature? Hasn't he admitted he's a traitor to his own leader? Must we do business with traitors now? How do we know this isn't more of his treason—some deep-laid plan, some sort of trap?'

Now General Kitab, as Haroun had observed, was as a rule the mildest of men, who liked nothing so much as a good argument; but on this occasion he went pink in the face and seemed to swell up slightly. 'Hang it all, your highness,' he finally said, 'I am in command here. Hold your tongue or you'll be on your way back to Gup City, and someone else will have to rescue your Batcheat on your behalf; and you wouldn't like that, I'd guess, spots and fogs, you wouldn't.' Blabbermouth looked delighted at this reprimand; Bolo looked murderous, but held his tongue.

Which was just as well, because Mudra's Shadow had responded to Bolo's outburst by going into a positive frenzy of changes, growing enormous, scratching itself all over, turning into the silhouette of a flame-breathing dragon, and then into other creatures: a gryphon, a basilisk, a manticore, a troll. And while the Shadow behaved in this agitated fashion, Mudra himself retreated a few steps, leant on a tree-stump and pretended to have grown very bored indeed, examining his fingernails, yawning, twiddling his thumbs. 'This Warrior and his Shadow are a fine team,' Haroun thought. 'They put on opposite acts, so nobody knows what they really feel; which may of course be a third thing completely.'

General Kitab approached Mudra with great, even exaggerated respect. 'Blow it all, Mudra, will you help us? It isn't going to be easy in the Darkness of Chup. We could do with a fellow like you. Mighty Warrior and all that. What do you say?'

Prince Bolo sulked at the edge of the clearing while Mudra paced and thought. Then he began to gesture once again. Rashid translated his 'words'.

'Yes, I will help,' the Shadow Warrior said. 'For the Cultmaster must surely be defeated. But there is a decision you must make.'

'I bet I know what it is,' Blabbermouth hissed at Haroun. 'It's the *same one* that should have been made before we even *set out*: what do we save first? Batcheat or the Ocean? —By the way,' she added, blushing slightly, 'isn't he *something*? Isn't he *wicked, awesome, sharp*? —Mudra, I *mean*.'

'I know who you mean,' said Haroun, with a pang of what might have been jealousy. 'He's okay, I suppose.'

'*Okay?*' hissed Blabbermouth. 'Only *okay*? How can you even *say* . . .'

But here she broke off, because Mudra's 'words' were being translated by Rashid. 'As I told you, there are now two Khattam-Shuds. One of them, at this very moment, has Princess Batcheat captive in the Citadel of Chup, and is planning to sew up her lips on the Feast of Bezaban. The other, as you should know, is in the Old Zone, where he is plotting the ruination of the Ocean of the Streams of Story.'

An immense stubbornness came over Prince Bolo of Gup. 'Say what you will, General,' he cried, 'but a Person must come before an Ocean, no matter how great the peril to both! It must be Batcheat first; Batcheat, my love, my only girl. Her cherry lips must be saved from the Cultmaster's needle, and without further delay! What are you people? Have you not blood in your veins? General, and you, too, Sir Mudra: are you men or . . . or . . . Shadows?'

'There is no need to insult Shadows any further,' Mudra's Shadow gestured with quiet dignity. (Bolo ignored it.)

'Very well,' General Kitab agreed. 'Rot it all, very well. But we must send someone to investigate the Old Zone situation. But whom? —Now let me see . . . Harrumph . . .'

It was at this instant that Haroun cleared his throat.

'I'll go,' he volunteered.

All eyes turned to stare at him as he stood there in his red nightshirt with the purple patches, feeling fairly ridiculous. 'Hmm? What's that you say?' Prince Bolo irritably demanded.

'Once you thought my father was spying for Khattam-Shud against you,' Haroun said. 'Now, if you and the General wish, I'll spy for you upon Khattam-Shud, or his Shadow, whichever of them is down there in the Old Zone, poisoning the Ocean.'

'And why—stap and blast me!—d'you volunteer for this dangerous job?' General Kitab wanted to know. *Good question*, Haroun thought. *I must be a very great fool.* But what he said aloud was this:

'Well, sir, it's like this. All my life I've heard about the wonderful Sea of Stories, and Water Genies, and everything; but I started believing only when I saw Iff in my bathroom the other night. And now that I've actually come to Kahani and seen with my own eyes how beautiful the Ocean is, with its Story Streams in colours whose names I don't even know, and its Floating Gardeners and Plentimaw Fishes and all, well, it turns out I may be too late, because the whole Ocean's going to be dead any minute if we don't do something. And it turns out that I don't like the idea of that, sir, not one bit. I don't like the idea that all the good stories in the world will go wrong for ever and ever, or just die. As I say, I only just started believing in the Ocean, but maybe it isn't too late for me to do my bit.'

There, he thought, *you've really done it now: made yourself look a complete idiot.* But Blabbermouth was looking at him in much the same way as she'd been staring at Mudra for some time, and that was pleasant, it couldn't be denied. And then he caught sight of his father's expression, and *oh no*, he thought, *I know exactly what he's going to say* . . .

'There's more to you, young Haroun Khalifa, than meets the blinking eye,' said Rashid.

'Forget it,' mumbled Haroun furiously. 'Forget I even *spoke.*'

Prince Bolo strode over and thumped Haroun on the back, leaving him winded. 'Out of the question!' Bolo was shouting. 'Forget you spoke? Young man, it will never be forgotten! General, I ask you: is this not the perfect fellow for the job? For he is, like me, a slave to Love.' Here

Haroun avoided looking at Blabbermouth, and blushed.

'Yes, indeed!' Prince Bolo continued, striding about and waving his arms in a dashing (and somewhat foolish) way. 'Just as my great passion, my *Amour*, leads me to Batcheat, always towards Batcheat, so this boy's destiny is to rescue what *he* loves: that is, the Ocean of Stories.'

'Very well,' General Kitab gave in. 'Young master Haroun, you will be our spy. Drat it all! You deserve it. Take your pick of companions, and begone.' His voice sounded gruff, as if he were hiding his worries beneath a façade of sternness. 'That's finished it,' Haroun thought. 'Too late to back out now.'

'Keep a sharp look out! Skulk in the shadows! See without being seen!' cried Bolo, dramatically. 'In a way, you'll be a Shadow Warrior, too.'

~ ~ ~

To reach the Old Zone of Kahani it was necessary to travel south through the Twilight Strip, hugging the shoreline of the Land of Chup, until that dark and silent continent was left behind, and the Southern Polar Ocean of Kahani stretched in every direction. Haroun and Iff the Water Genie set off on this route within an hour of Haroun's volunteering. Their chosen companions were the Plentimaw Fishes, Goopy and Bagha, who bubbled along in their wake, and the gnarled old Floating Gardener, Mali, with his lilac lips and hat of roots. Mali walked on the water at their side. (Haroun had wanted to take Blabbermouth, but a shyness overcame him, and besides, she seemed to want to stay with Mudra the Shadow Warrior. And Rashid had been needed to translate Mudra's Gesture Language to the General and the Prince.)

After several hours of high-speed travel through the Twilight Strip, they found themselves in the Southern Polar Ocean. Here the waters had lost even more of their colouring, and the water temperature had dropped even lower.

'We're going the right way! We can tell!'

'Before, it was filthy! Now it's Hell!'

said Goopy and Bagha, coughing and spluttering.

Mali loped along over the water's surface without any sign of discomfort. 'If that water is so badly poisoned, doesn't it hurt your feet?' Haroun asked him. Mali shook his head. 'Take more'n that. A little poison, bah. A little acid, pah. A Gardener's a tough old bird. It won't stop me.'

Then, to Haroun's surprise, he burst into a little, rough-voiced song:

> You can stop a cheque,
> You can stop a leak or three,
> You can stop traffic, but
> You can't stop me!

'What we are here to stop,' Haroun reminded him, adopting what he hoped was an authoritative, leader-like tone of voice, 'is the work of the Cultmaster, Khattam-Shud.'

'If it's true that there is a Wellspring, or Source of Stories, near the South Pole,' suggested Iff, 'then that's where Khattam-Shud will be, you can be sure of it.'

'Very well, then,' Haroun agreed. 'To the South Pole!'

The first disaster struck soon afterwards. Goopy and Bagha, uttering piteous whimpering noises, confessed that they couldn't go any further.

'Never thought it'd be so bad!'

'We have failed you! We feel sad!'

'I feel terrible! She feels worse!'

'We can hardly speak in verse.'

The waters of the Ocean were growing thicker by the mile, thicker and colder; many of the Streams of Story were full of a dark, slow-moving substance that looked like molasses. 'Whatever is doing this can't be very far away,' Haroun thought. To the Plentimaw Fishes he said sadly: 'Stay here and keep watch. We'll go on without you.' *Of course, even if there is danger, they won't be able to warn us,* Haroun realized, but the Plentimaw Fishes were already so miserable that he kept this thought to himself.

The light was poor now (they were at the very edge of the Twilight Strip, very near the hemisphere of Perpetual Darkness). They travelled on towards the Pole; and when Haroun saw a forest standing up from the Ocean, its tall growths waving in a light breeze, the absence of light added to the mystification. 'Land?' Haroun asked. 'Surely there's not meant to be any land here?'

'Neglected waters is what it is,' said Mali in disgust. 'Overgrown. Gone to weed. Run down. Nobody to keep the place in trim. It's a disgrace. Give me a year and the whole place'd look like new.' It was quite a speech for the Floating Gardener. He was plainly upset.

'We haven't got a year,' Haroun said. 'And I don't want to fly over it. Too easy to spot, and we couldn't take you with us, anyway.'

'Don't you go worrying about me,' said Mali. 'And don't be thinking about flying, either. I'll clear a way.' And with that, he put on a great burst of speed and disappeared into the floating jungle. A few moments later Haroun saw huge clumps of vegetation flying into the air, as Mali got to work. The creatures who lived in this weed-jungle rushed out in alarm: giant albino moths, large grey birds that were all bone and no meat, long whitish worms with heads like shovel blades. 'Even the wildlife is Old here,' Haroun thought. 'Will there be dinosaurs further in? —Well, not dinosaurs exactly, but the water-dwelling ones—that's right—ichthyosaurs.' The idea of seeing an ichthyosaur's head poking out of the water was both scary and exciting. 'Anyhow, they are vegetarians—*were* vegetarians,' he comforted himself. 'At least, I think so.'

Mali strode back across the water to give a progress report. 'Bit of weeding. Bit of pest control. Have a channel ready in no time.' And back in he went.

When the channel was clear, Haroun directed Butt the Hoopoe to enter. Mali was nowhere to be seen. 'Where have you got to?' Haroun called. 'This is no time for hide-and-seek.' But there was no reply.

It was a narrow channel, with roots and weeds still floating on the surface . . . and they were deep inside the heart of the weed-jungle when the second catastrophe occurred. Haroun heard a faint, hissing sound, and an instant later saw something enormous being thrown in their direction—something that looked like a colossal net, a net that had been spun out of the darkness itself. It fell over them, and held them tight.

'It is a Web of Night,' said Butt the Hoopoe usefully. 'A legendary Chupwala weapon. Struggle is useless; the more you fight, the harder it grips. Our goose, I regret to inform, is cooked.'

Haroun heard noises outside the Web of Night: hisses, little satisfied chuckles. And there were eyes, too, eyes staring through the net, eyes like Mudra's, with blacks instead of whites—but these eyes were not friendly in the least. —*And where was Mali?*

'So we're prisoners already,' Haroun fumed. 'Some hero I turned out to be.'

9

The Dark Ship

They were being pulled slowly forwards. Their captors, whose shadowy shapes Haroun started to be able to make out as his eyes became accustomed to the darkness, were drawing the Web along by invisible but powerful super-strings of some sort. Forward to what, though? Here Haroun's imagination failed him. All he could see in his mind's eye was a huge black hole, yawning at him like a great mouth, and sucking him slowly in.

'Up the creek, pretty pickle, had our chips,' Iff disconsolately remarked. Butt the Hoopoe was in an equally cheerless state of mind. 'To Khattam-Shud we go, all neatly wrapped and tied up like a present!' the Hoopoe wailed without moving its beak. 'Then it's zap, bam, phutt, finito for us all. There he sits at the heart of darkness—at the bottom of a black hole, so they say—and he eats light, eats it raw with his bare hands, and lets none of it escape. —He eats words, too. —And he can be in two places at one time, and there is no getting away. Woe is us! Alas, alack-a-day! *Hai-hai-hai!*'

'*You're* a fine pair of companions and no mistake,' Haroun said as light-heartedly as he could manage. To Butt the Hoopoe he added, 'Some machine! You swallow every spooky story you hear, even the ones you find in other people's minds. That black hole, for example: I was thinking about that, and you just pinched it and then let it frighten you. Honestly, Hoopoe, pull yourself together.'

'How to pull myself, together or anywhere else,' Butt the Hoopoe lamented without moving its beak, 'when other persons, Chupwala persons, are pulling me wherever they desire?'

'Look down,' Iff broke in. 'Look down at the Ocean.'

The thick, dark poison was everywhere now, obliterating the colours of the Streams of Story, which Haroun could no longer tell apart. A cold, clammy feeling rose up from the water, which was near freezing point, 'as cold as death', Haroun found himself thinking. Iff's grief began to overflow. 'It's our own fault,' he wept. 'We are the Guardians of the Ocean, and we didn't guard it. Look at the Ocean, look at it! The oldest stories ever made, and look at them now. We let them rot, we abandoned them, long before this poisoning. We lost touch with our beginnings, with our roots, our Wellspring, our Source. Boring, we said, not in demand, surplus to requirements. And now, look, just look! No colour, no life, no nothing. Spoilt!'

How this sight would have horrified Mali, Haroun thought; perhaps Mali most of all. But of the Floating Gardener there was still no trace. 'Probably trussed up like us in another Web of Night,' Haroun guessed. 'But O, what wouldn't I give to see his gnarled old root-body running along beside us now, and to hear that soft flowery voice speaking such rough and infrequent words.'

The poisoned waters lapped at Butt the Hoopoe's sides—and then splashed suddenly higher, as the Web of Night was brought to an abrupt halt. Iff and Haroun, acting by reflex, jerked their feet away from the splashing liquid, and one of the Water Genie's attractively embroidered and twirly-pointed slippers fell (from, to be precise, his left foot) into the Ocean; where, quick as a blink, with a fizz and a hiss and a burble and a gurgle, it was instantly eaten away, right down to the tip of its twirly toe. Haroun was impressed, in a horrified way. 'The poison is so concentrated here that it behaves like a powerful acid,' he remarked. 'Hoopoe, you must be made of tough stuff. Iff, you're lucky it was just your slipper that fell in, and not you.'

'Don't sound too pleased,' Butt the Hoopoe said moodily without moving its beak. 'Who knows what's in store for us, up ahead?'

'Well, thanks very much,' Haroun rejoined. 'Another happy notion from you.'

But he was worrying about Mali. The Floating Gardener had actually been walking over the surface of this concentrated poison. He was a tough old creature, but could he withstand its acid-like power? Haroun had an awful mental image of Mali sinking slowly into the Ocean, where with a fizz and a hiss and a burble and a gurgle . . . he shook his head. No time for such negative thoughts now.

The Web of Night was pulled away, and as the faint twilight returned Haroun saw that they had reached a large clearing in the weed-jungle. Just a short distance away was what looked like a wall of night. 'That must be the beginning of the Perpetual Darkness,' Haroun thought. 'We must be at the very edge of it now.'

Only a few roots and weeds, most of them badly burned and corroded by the poison-acid, floated on the surface of the Ocean here. There was still no sign of Mali, and Haroun continued to fear the worst.

A party of thirteen Chupwalas had surrounded Butt the Hoopoe, and pointed menacing-looking weapons at Iff and

Haroun. They all had the same strange reversed eyes, with white pupils instead of black ones, bland grey irises instead of coloured ones, and blackness where the whites should have been, which Haroun had first seen on the face of Mudra. But, unlike the Shadow Warrior, these Chupwalas were scrawny, snivelling, weaselly-looking types wearing black hooded cloaks adorned with the special insignia of Cultmaster Khattam-Shud's personal guards—that is, the Sign of the Zipped Lips. 'They look like a gang of office clerks in fancy dress,' Haroun thought. 'But they're not to be underestimated; they are dangerous, no question about it at all.'

The Chupwalas clustered around Butt the Hoopoe and stared curiously at Haroun, which was annoying. They were riding what looked like large, dark sea-horses, which seemed to be just as puzzled by the Earth boy's presence as their riders. 'For information only,' Butt the Hoopoe revealed, 'these dark horses are machines also. But a dark horse, as is well known, is unreliable, and not to be trusted.'

Haroun wasn't listening.

He had just seen that the wall of night, which he had thought to be the beginning of the Perpetual Darkness, was no such thing. It was in fact a colossal ship, a vast ark-like vessel standing at anchor in the clearing. 'That's where they'll be taking us,' he understood with a sinking heart. 'It must be the flagship of the Cultmaster, Khattam-Shud.' But when he opened his mouth to say as much to Iff, he found that fear had dried his throat and all that came out of his mouth was a strange croaking noise:

'Ark,' he croaked, pointing to the dark ship. 'Ark, ark.'

~ ~ ~

Gangways with railings slanted down along the side of the
Dark Ship. The Chupwalas brought them to the foot of one
such gangway, and here Haroun and Iff had to leave Butt
the Hoopoe behind and begin the long climb to the deck.
As Haroun climbed, he heard a piteous cry, and turned to
see the Hoopoe protesting, without moving its beak, 'But
but but *that* you must not take—no, you can't—it's my
brain!' Two cloaked Chupwalas were on Butt's back,
unscrewing the top of the Hoopoe's head. From the head
cavity they removed a small, dully gleaming metal box,
emitting, as they did so, a series of short, satisfied hisses. And
then they simply left Butt the Hoopoe floating there, its
circuits disconnected, its memory cells and command
module removed. It looked like a broken toy. 'Oh,
Hoopoe,' Haroun thought, 'I'm sorry I ever teased you
about being only a machine! You're the best and bravest
machine that ever there was, and I'll get your brain back for
you, just see if I don't.' But he knew it was an empty
promise, because after all he had troubles of his own.

They climbed on. Then Iff, who was behind Haroun,
stumbled badly, seemed on the verge of falling, and grabbed
Haroun's hand, apparently to steady himself. Haroun felt the
Water Genie pushing something small and hard into his
palm. He closed his fist over it.

'A little emergency something, courtesy of P2C2E

House,' Iff whispered. 'Maybe you'll get a chance to use it.'

The Chupwalas were ahead of them and behind as well. 'What is it?' Haroun muttered in his lowest voice.

'Bite the end off,' Iff whispered, 'and it gives you two full minutes of bright, bright light. So it's called a Bite-a-Lite, for obvious reasons. Hide it under your tongue.'

'What about you?' Haroun whispered back. 'Have you got one as well?' But Iff did not reply, and Haroun understood that the Water Genie had given Haroun the only such device he possessed. 'I can't take it, it's not fair,' Haroun whispered, but now one of the Chupwalas hissed at him so terrifyingly that he decided he'd better keep quiet for a while. Up, up they climbed, wondering what the Cultmaster had in mind.

They climbed past a row of portholes, and Haroun let out an astonished gasp, because pouring out of the portholes came *darkness*—darkness glowing in the twilight the way light does from a window in the evening. The Chupwalas had invented artificial darkness, just as other people had artificial light! Inside the Dark Ship, Haroun guessed, there must be lightbulbs—except they'd have to be called 'darkbulbs'—producing this strange darkness, so that the reversed eyes of the Chupwalas (which would be blinded by brightness) could see properly (although he, Haroun, would be unable to see anything at all). 'Darkness you can switch on and off,' Haroun marvelled. 'What a notion, I swear.'

They reached the deck.

Now Haroun realized just how enormous the ship was. In that dim light it seemed that the deck was literally infinite;

certainly Haroun could not see clearly all the way to the bow, or indeed to the stern. 'It must be a mile long!' he exclaimed, and if it was a mile long, then it was probably at least half a mile wide.

'Outsize, super-colossal, *big*,' Iff morosely agreed.

Arranged in a sort of chequerboard pattern on the deck were great numbers of gigantic black tanks or cauldrons, each with its own team of maintenance operatives. Pipes and ducts led into and out of each of these, and there were ladders up their sides. Small mechanical cranes were positioned by each cauldron, too, with buckets hanging from maliciously sharp-looking hooks. 'Those must be the poison tanks,' Haroun guessed; and he was right. The cauldrons were brim-full of the black poisons that were murdering the Ocean of Stories—poisons in their most potent, pure, undiluted form. 'It's a factory ship,' Haroun thought with a shudder, 'and what it makes is far, far worse than the sadness factories back home.'

The largest object on the deck of the Dark Ship was another crane. This one towered above the deck like a tall building, and from its mighty arm Haroun saw immense chains descending into the waters. Whatever hung at the end of these chains, down below the Ocean's surface, must indeed be of astonishing size and weight; but Haroun had no idea of what it was.

What struck Haroun first about the Dark Ship and everything upon it was a quality of what he could only call *shadowiness*. In spite of the mammoth scale of the ship itself, and the terrifying size and number of the poison tanks and the giant crane, Haroun kept having the notion that the whole affair was somehow *impermanent*, that there was something not quite fixed or certain about it all, as if some great sorcerer had somehow managed to build the whole thing out of shadows—to give shadows a solidity that Haroun had no idea they could possess. 'But this is all too fanciful for words,' he told himself. 'A boat made out of shadows? A shadow-ship? Don't be nuts.' But the idea kept nagging at him, and wouldn't let go. *Look at the edges of everything here*, said a voice in his head. *The edges of the poison tanks, the crane, the ship itself. Don't they look, well, fuzzy? That's what shadows are like; even when they're sharp, they're never as sharp-edged as real, substantial things.*

As for the Chupwalas, all of whom belonged to the Union of the Zipped Lips, and were the Cultmaster's most devoted servants—well, Haroun kept being struck by how ordinary they were, and how monotonous was the work they had been given. There were hundreds of them in their Zipped Lips cloaks and hoods, attending to the tanks and cranes on the deck, performing a series of mindless, routine jobs: checking dials, tightening joints, switching the tanks' stirring mechanisms on and off again, swabbing the decks. It was all as boring as could be; and yet—as Haroun kept having to remind himself—what these scurrying, cloaked, weaselly, scrawny, snivelling clerical types were actually up to was nothing less than the destruction of the Ocean of the Streams of Story itself! 'How weird,' Haroun said to Iff, 'that the worst things of all can look so *normal* and, well, *dull.*'

'Normal, he calls this,' Iff sighed. 'The boy is crazy, bananas, out to *lunch*.'

Their captors pushed them towards a large hatchway in which were set two tall black doors bearing the Zipped Lips symbol of Khattam-Shud. All this was done in total silence, except for the eerie hissing sound that the Chupwalas used instead of speech; and when they were a few feet away from the double doors, they were stopped, and held by the arms. The double doors opened. 'This is it,' Haroun told himself.

Through the doors came a skinny, scrawny, measly, weaselly, snivelling clerical type, exactly like all the others. But also unlike: because as soon as he appeared, every Chupwala in sight began to bow and scrape as energetically as possible; for this unimpressive creature was none other than the notorious and terrifying Cultmaster of Bezaban, Khattam-Shud, the big bogeyman himself!

'*That's* him? That's *him*?' Haroun thought, with a kind of disappointment. 'This little minging fellow? What an anti-climax.'

Now came another surprise: the Cultmaster began to speak. Khattam-Shud neither hissed like his minions, nor croaked and gurgled like Mudra the Shadow Warrior, but spoke clearly, in a dull, inflexionless voice, a voice nobody would ever have remembered if it hadn't belonged to so powerful and terrifying a Personage. 'Spies,' said Khattam-Shud dully. 'What a tiresome melodrama. A Water Genie from Gup City, and something more unusual: a young fellow from, if I'm not mistaken, *down there*.'

'So much for all your Silence nonsense,' said Iff

with considerable courage. 'Isn't it typical, couldn't you have guessed it, wouldn't you have known: the Grand Panjandrum himself does exactly what he wants to forbid everyone else to do. His followers sew up their lips and he talks and talks like billy-o.'

Khattam-Shud pretended to ignore these remarks. Haroun stared at him, looking particularly at the edges of the Cultmaster's body, and finally he was sure: it was there, that same fuzziness, that wobbliness he had spotted in the Dark Ship itself: *shadowiness*, he had called it, and he'd been right. 'No doubt about it,' he decided. 'This is the Cultmaster's Shadow, which he learnt how to detach. He has sent the Shadow here, and remains in the Citadel of Chup.' Where the Guppee forces, along with Haroun's father Rashid, must be heading even now.

If he was right, and this really was the shadow-become-human rather than the man-grown-shadowy, then Khattam-Shud's sorcery was very powerful indeed; for the figure of the Cultmaster was entirely three-dimensional, with eyes moving visibly in its head. 'I never in my life saw such a shadow,' Haroun had to admit; but his conviction that it was, indeed, the Cultmaster's Shadow-Self that had come to the Old Zone in this Dark Ship continued to grow.

The Chupwala who had removed Butt the Hoopoe's brain-box stepped forward and gave it to Khattam-Shud with a bow of the head. The Cultmaster commenced tossing the little metal cube lightly into the air, murmuring, 'Now we shall see about their Processes Too Complicated To Explain. Once this is taken apart, I'll explain those processes, never fear.'

Just then Haroun had a notion that made his head spin. *Khattam-Shud reminded him of someone.* 'I know him,' he thought in utter amazement. 'I've met him somewhere before. It's impossible, but there it is: he's very, very familiar.'

The Cultmaster came over and peered into Haroun's face. 'What brought you up here, eh?' he asked in his dull, dull voice. '*Stories*, I suppose.' He said the word 'stories' as if it were the rudest, most contemptible word in the language. 'Well, look where *stories* have landed you now. You follow me? What starts with *stories* ends with spying, and that's a serious charge, boy, no charge more serious. You'd have done better to keep your feet on the ground but you had your head in the air. You'd have done better to stick to Facts, but you were stuffed with *stories*. You'd have done better to have stayed home, but up you came. *Stories* make trouble. An Ocean of *Stories* is an Ocean of Trouble. Answer me this: what's the use of *stories* that aren't even true?'

'I know you,' Haroun shouted. 'You're him. You're Mr Sengupta and you stole my mother and you left the fat lady behind and you're a snivelling, drivelling, mingy, stingy, measly, weasely *clerk*. Where are you hiding her? Maybe she's a prisoner on this ship! Come on; hand her over.'

Iff the Water Genie held Haroun kindly by the shoulders. He was shaking with anger and other emotions, and Iff waited until he had calmed down. 'Haroun, lad, it's not the same guy,' Iff gently said. 'Maybe he looks the same, the spitting image, the exact double; but, believe me, boy, this is the Cultmaster of Bezaban, Khattam-Shud.'

Khattam-Shud, in his clerky way, seemed quite unperturbed. His right hand continued, absently, to toss Butt the Hoopoe's brain-box into the air. Finally he spoke in that droning, sleepy-making voice of his. '*Stories* have warped the boy's brain,' he pronounced solemnly. 'Now he daydreams and spouts rubbish. Insulting, abusive child. Why would I have the slightest interest in your mother? *Stories* have made you incapable of seeing who stands before you. *Stories* have made you believe that a Personage such as Cultmaster Khattam-Shud ought to look like . . . *this*.'

Haroun and Iff both cried out in shock as Khattam-Shud changed his shape. The Cultmaster grew and grew before their appalled, astonished eyes, until he was one hundred and one feet tall, with one hundred and one heads, each of which had three eyes and a protruding tongue of flame; and a hundred and one arms, one hundred of which were holding enormous black swords, while the one hundred and first tossed Butt the Hoopoe's brain-box casually into the air . . . and then, with a little sigh, Khattam-Shud shrank back into his earlier, clerkish form. 'Showing off,' he shrugged. '*Stories* go in for such displays, but they are unnecessary and inefficient, too. —Spies, spies,' he mused. 'Well, you must see what you came to see. Though obviously you will not be able to make your report.'

He turned, and began to slink back towards the black doors. 'Bring them,' he commanded, and was gone. Chupwala soldiers surrounded Haroun and Iff, and pushed them through the doors. They found themselves at the head of a wide, black flight of stairs, which disappeared down and away into the pitch blackness of the interior of the ship.

10

Haroun's Wish

As Haroun and Iff stood there at the top of the stairs, the absolute darkness created by thousands of 'darkbulbs' suddenly disappeared, to be replaced by the dim twilight. Khattam-Shud had ordered the big switch-off, so that he could taunt his captives by showing them the extent of his power. Haroun and Iff could see their way now, and began to walk down into the belly of that immense ship. All around them, Chupwalas were putting on really rather fashionable wrap-around dark glasses, to help them see better in the increased level of light. 'Now they look like office clerks pretending to be rock stars,' thought Haroun.

He could now see that, below decks, the Dark Ship was a single voluminous cavern, around which walkways ran at seven different levels, connected by stairways and ladders; and it was full of machinery. And what machines they were! 'Far Too Complicated To Describe,' Iff murmured. What a whirring of whirrers and stirring of stirrers, what ranks of lifters and banks of sifters, what a humming of squeezers and thrumming of freezers was there! Khattam-Shud waited for them on a high catwalk, tossing Butt the Hoopoe's brain idly from hand to hand. No sooner had Haroun and Iff (and their guards, of course) reached him than he began, drily, to explain everything.

Haroun forced himself to listen, even though the Cultmaster's voice was boring enough to send a person to sleep in ten seconds flat. 'These are the Poison Blenders,' Khattam-Shud was saying. 'We must make a great many poisons, because each and every story in the Ocean needs to be ruined in a different way. To ruin a happy story, you must make it sad. To ruin an action drama, you must make it move too slowly. To ruin a mystery you must make the criminal's identity obvious even to the most stupid audience. To ruin a love story you must turn it into a tale of hate. To ruin a tragedy you must make it capable of inducing helpless laughter.'

'To ruin an Ocean of Stories,' muttered Iff the Water Genie, 'you must add a Khattam-Shud.'

'Say what you like,' the Cultmaster told him. 'Say it while you can.'

He went on with his terrifying explanations: 'Now the fact is that I personally have discovered that *for every story there is an anti-story*. I mean that every story—and so every Stream of Story—has a *shadow-self*, and if you pour this anti-story into the story, the two cancel each other out, and bingo! End of story. —Now then: you see here the proof that I have found a way of synthesizing these anti-stories, these shadow-tales. Yes! I can mix them up right here, in laboratory conditions, and produce a most efficient concentrated poison that none of the stories in your precious Ocean can resist. These concentrated poisons are what we have been releasing, one by one, into the Ocean. You have seen how thick the poison is here—thick as treacle. That's because all the shadow-tales are packed together so closely. Gradually, they will flow out along the currents of the Ocean, each anti-story seeking out its victim. Each day we synthesize and release new poisons! Each day we murder new tales! Soon now, soon, the Ocean will be dead—cold and dead. When black ice freezes over its surface, my victory will be complete.'

'But why do you hate stories so much?' Haroun blurted, feeling stunned. 'Stories are fun . . . '

'The world, however, is not for Fun,' Khattam-Shud replied. 'The world is for Controlling.'

'Which world?' Haroun made himself ask.

'Your world, my world, all worlds,' came the reply. 'They are all there to be Ruled. And inside every single story, inside every Stream in the Ocean, there lies a world, a story-world, that I cannot Rule at all. And that is the reason why.'

Now the Cultmaster pointed out the refrigeration machines that kept the poisons, the anti-stories, at the necessary low temperatures. And he pointed out the filtration machines that removed all dirt and impurities from the poisons, so that they were one hundred per cent pure, one hundred per cent deadly. And he explained why, as part of the manufacturing process, the poison had to spend some time in the cauldrons up on deck—'like all good wine, the anti-stories improve if they are permitted to "breathe" for a while in the open air before being released'. After eleven minutes of this, Haroun stopped listening. He followed Khattam-Shud and Iff along the high catwalk until they reached another part of the ship, in which Chupwalas were putting together large, mysterious segments of what looked like hard, black rubber.

'Now this,' said the Cultmaster (and something in his voice made Haroun pay attention), 'is where we are building the Plug.'

'What Plug?' cried Iff, as an appalling idea took shape in

his thoughts. 'You can't mean . . .'

'You will have seen the giant crane up on deck,' said Khattam-Shud in his most monotonous voice. 'You will have noted the chains going down into the waters. At the other end of those chains, Chupwala divers are rapidly assembling the largest and most efficient Plug ever constructed. It is almost complete, little spies, almost complete; and so, in a few days, we shall be able to put it to good use. We are going to Plug the Wellspring itself, the Source of Stories, which lies directly beneath this ship on the ocean-bed. As long as that Source remains unplugged, fresh, unpoisoned, renewing Story Waters will pour upwards into the Ocean, and our work will only be half-done. But when it's Plugged! Ah, then the Ocean will lose all its power to resist my anti-stories, and the end will come very soon. And then, Water Genie: what will there be for you Guppees to do, but to accept the victory of Bezaban?'

'Never,' said Iff, but he didn't sound very convincing.

'How do the divers enter the poisoned waters without being hurt?' Haroun asked. Khattam-Shud smiled a dry little smile. 'Paying attention again, I see,' he said. 'The obvious answer is that they wear protective clothing. Here, in this cupboard, are numbers of poison-proof suits.'

He led them on, past the Plug assembly zone, to an area occupied by the largest machine in the entire ship.

'And this,' said Khattam-Shud, almost permitting a note of pride to enter his dull, flat voice, 'is our Generator.'

'What does that do?' asked Haroun, who had never been of a particularly scientific turn of mind.

'It is a device for converting mechanical energy into electrical energy by means of electromagnetic induction,' replied Khattam-Shud, 'if you *must* know.'

Haroun was unabashed. 'Do you mean it's where your power supply comes from?' he persevered.

'Precisely,' the Cultmaster replied. 'I see that education is not quite at a standstill on Earth.'

At this point something wholly unexpected occurred.

Through an open porthole a few paces from the Cultmaster, bizarre rooty tendrils began to enter the Dark Ship. They came in at high speed, a great unformed mass of vegetation, among which was a single, lilac-coloured flower. Haroun's heart gave a great leap of joy. 'M . . .' he began, but then he held his tongue.

Mali had escaped capture (as Haroun later learned) by reassuming the appearance of a bunch of lifeless roots. He had floated slowly towards the Dark Ship, and then used the suction pads on several of the tendrils which made up his body to climb up the outside of the vessel like a creeper. Now, as he completed his dramatic entry and whirled himself in a trice into his more familiar Mali-shape, the alarm was sounded: 'Intruder! Intruder alert!'

'Switch on the darkness!' screeched Khattam-Shud, his usual, insipid manner falling away from him like a mask. Mali began to move at high speed in the direction of the Generator. Before the 'darkbulbs' had been switched on, he had reached the gigantic machine, having eluded numbers of Chupwala guards whose eyesight wasn't what it should have been, owing to the dim twilight (and in spite of their really rather fashionable wrap-around dark glasses). Without pausing for an instant, the Floating Gardener leapt into the air, disassembling his body as he did so, and flung roots and tendrils all over the Generator, getting into every nook and cranny of the machine.

There now began a series of loud bangs and crashes, as circuits blew and cog-wheels broke, and the mighty Generator came to a juddering halt. The ship's entire power supply was cut off at once: stirrers stopped stirring and whirrers stopped whirring; blenders stopped blending and menders stopped mending; squeezers stopped squeezing and freezers stopped freezing; poison-storers stopped storing and poison-pourers stopped their pouring. The entire operation was at a standstill! 'Hurray, Mali!' Haroun cheered. 'Nice work, mister, too good!'

Chupwala guards now attacked Mali in large numbers, pulling at him with their bare hands, hacking at him with axes and swords; but a creature tough enough to withstand the concentrated poisons which Khattam-Shud had been pouring into the Ocean of Stories wasn't bothered by such flea-bites. He hung on to the Generator until he was sure it was ruined beyond hope of quick repair, and, as he clung to that machine, he began in his rough Gardener's way to sing through the lilac flower that served him for a mouth:

> You can chop a flower-bush,
> You can chop a tree,
> You can chop liver, but
> You can't chop me!

You can chop and change,
You can chop in ka-ra-tee,
You can chop suey, but
You can't chop me!

'Okay,' Haroun told himself, seeing that Khattam-Shud's attention was wholly focused on the Floating Gardener, 'come on, Haroun; it's your turn, and it's now or never.'

The 'little emergency something', the Bite-a-Lite, was still hidden under his tongue. Quickly, he put it between his teeth, and bit.

The light that poured out from his mouth was as bright as the sun! The Chupwalas all around him were blinded, and broke their vows of silence to shriek and utter curses as they clutched their eyes. Even Khattam-Shud reeled back from the glare.

Haroun moved as fast as he'd ever moved in his life. He took the Bite-a-Lite out of his mouth and held it over his head; now the light poured in every direction, illuminating the entire vast interior of that massive ship. 'Those Eggheads back at P2C2E House certainly know a thing or two,' Haroun thought in wonderment. But he was running now, because the seconds were ticking away. As he passed Cultmaster Khattam-Shud he stuck out his free hand and grabbed Butt the Hoopoe's brain-box from the Cultmaster's hand. He ran on, until he reached the cupboard containing the protective clothing for the Chupwala divers. A minute had already passed.

Haroun shoved Butt the Hoopoe's brain into a pocket of

his nightshirt and began to wrestle his way into the diving-suit. He had placed the Bite-a-Lite on a convenient railing, so that he could use both hands. 'But how does this thing go on?' he groaned in frustration as the diving-suit refused to slip on smoothly. (Trying to pull it over a long red nightshirt with purple patches didn't exactly help.) The seconds ticked away.

Although he was frantically busy with the diving-suit, Haroun did notice a number of things: he noticed, for example, that Khattam-Shud had personally grabbed Iff the Water Genie by his blue whiskers. He also noticed that *none of the Chupwalas had shadows*! That could mean only one thing: Khattam-Shud had shown his most trusted devotees, the Union of the Zipped Lips, how to detach themselves from their shadows, just like himself. 'So they are all shadows here,' he understood. 'The boat, the Zipped Lips gang, and Khattam-Shud himself. Everything and everyone here is a Shadow made Solid, except for Iff, Mali, Butt the Hoopoe, and me.'

The third thing he noticed was this: as the brilliant light of the Bite-a-Lite filled the interior of the Dark Ship, the whole vessel seemed to quiver for a moment, to become a little less solid, a little more shadowy; and the Chupwalas, too, trembled, and their edges softened and they began to lose their three-dimensional form . . . 'If only the sun would come out,' Haroun realized, 'they'd all melt away, they'd become flat and shapeless, like the shadows they really are!'

But there was no sunlight to be found anywhere in that dim twilight; and the seconds were running out; and just as the two minutes of light came to an end, Haroun zipped up the diving-suit, pulled on the goggles, and dived head-first out of a porthole, towards the poisoned Ocean.

~ ~ ~

As he hit the water, a terrible feeling of hopelessness overcame him. 'What are you going to do, Haroun?' he asked himself. 'Swim all the way back to Gup City?'

He fell through the waters of the Ocean for a long, long time, and the deeper he went the less filthy the Story Streams were, and the easier it was to see.

He saw the Plug. Teams of Chupwala divers were at work, bolting pieces on to it. Fortunately, they were too busy to notice Haroun . . . The Plug was about the size of a football stadium, and very roughly oval. Its edges were raggedy and uneven, however, because it was being constructed to fit precisely into the Wellspring, or Source of Stories, and the two shapes, Plug and Wellspring, had to be a perfect match.

Haroun continued to fall . . . and then, wonder of wonders, he caught sight of the Source itself.

The Source of Stories was a hole or chasm or crater in the sea-bed, and through that hole, as Haroun watched, the glowing flow of pure, unpolluted stories came bubbling up from the very heart of Kahani. There were so many Streams of Story, of so many different colours, all pouring out of the Source at once, that it looked like a huge underwater fountain of shining white light. In that moment Haroun understood that if he could prevent the Source from being Plugged, everything would eventually be all right again. The renewed Streams of Story would cleanse the polluted waters, and Khattam-Shud's plan would fail.

Now he was at the low point of his plunge, and as he began to rise towards the surface he thought with all his heart: 'Oh, I wish, how I wish, there was something I could do.'

At that moment, seemingly by chance, his hand brushed against the thigh of his diving-suit; and he felt a bulge in the nightshirt pocket beneath. 'That's strange,' he thought, 'I'm sure I put Butt the Hoopoe's brain-box in the pocket on the other side.' Then he remembered what was in that pocket, what had lain there, completely forgotten, ever since he first arrived on Kahani; and in a flash he knew that there was something he could do, after all.

~ ~ ~

He returned to the surface with a whoosh, and lifted up his goggles to take several gulps of air (while taking care not to let the poisoned waters of the Ocean lap his face). As luck would have it—'and it's high time I had some luck' Haroun thought—he had surfaced right next to the gangway to which the disabled Butt the Hoopoe had been tethered; while the search-party which Khattam-Shud had sent out to recapture him was heading off across the clearing towards the weed-jungle, using torches fitted with 'darkbulbs' to help them see. Long beams of absolute pitch-blackness raked the weed-jungle. 'Good,' thought Haroun. 'I hope they search in that direction for a long time.' He hauled himself out of the water on to the gangway, unzipped his diving-suit, and took out Butt the Hoopoe's brain-box. 'I'm no engineer, Hoopoe,' he murmured, 'but let's see if I can plug this back in.'

The Chupwalas had fortunately neglected to screw the lid of the Hoopoe's head down again. Haroun climbed aboard Butt as stealthily as he could, lifted the lid, and looked inside.

There were three loose leads inside the empty brain cavity. Haroun quickly found the three points on the brain-box to which they had to be connected. But which went where? 'Oh well,' he told himself, 'here goes nothing,' and he plugged the three leads in at random.

Butt the Hoopoe emitted an alarming sequence of giggles and quacks and other strange noises. Then it burst into a weird little song:

> You must sing, a–down a–down,
> And you call him a–down–a.

'I've connected it up wrong, and I've sent it insane,' Haroun panicked. Aloud he said: 'Hoopoe, be quiet, *please*.'

'Look, look! A mouse. Peace, peace! This piece of toasted cheese will do it,' ranted Butt the Hoopoe, nonsensically. '*No problem*.'

Hurriedly, Haroun disconnected the three leads, and changed them round. This time Butt the Hoopoe began to buck and bounce like a wild horse, and Haroun jerked the leads out to prevent himself from being bucked off into the Ocean. 'Third time lucky, I hope,' he thought, and with a deep breath, reconnected the leads again.

'So what took you so long?' said Butt in its familiar voice. 'All fixed up now. Let's go. Va-va-voom!'

'Hold your horses, Hoopoe,' Haroun whispered. 'You just sit there and pretend you're still brainless. I've got something else to do.'

And now, at last, he reached into his other nightshirt pocket, and drew out a small bottle made of many-faceted crystal, with a little golden cap. The bottle was still half-full of the magical golden liquid which Iff the Water Genie had offered him what seemed like years earlier: *Wishwater*. 'The harder you wish, the better it works,' Iff had told him. 'Do serious business, and the Wishwater will do serious business for you.'

'This may take more than eleven minutes,' Haroun whispered to Butt the Hoopoe, 'but I'm going to do it all right. Hoopoe, you just watch me try.' And so saying, he unscrewed the golden lid and drank the Wishwater down to the last drop.

All he could see was a golden light, which had wrapped itself around him like a shawl . . . 'I wish,' thought Haroun Khalifa, squeezing his eyes tightly shut, wishing with every fibre of his being, 'I wish this Moon, Kahani, to turn, so that it's no longer half in light and half in darkness . . . I wish it to turn, this very instant, in such a way that the sun shines down on the Dark Ship, the full, hot, noonday sun.'

'That's some wish,' said Butt the Hoopoe's voice admiringly. 'This will be pretty interesting. It's your willpower against the Processes Too Complicated To Explain.'

~ ~ ~

The minutes passed: one, two, three, four, five. Haroun lay stretched out on the back of Butt the Hoopoe, oblivious of time, oblivious of everything except his wish. In the weed-jungle, the Chupwala searchers decided they were looking in the wrong place, and turned back towards the Dark Ship. Their 'darkbulbed' torches sent probing beams of darkness through the twilight. By chance, none of these beams fell upon Butt the Hoopoe. More minutes passed: six, seven, eight, nine, ten.

Eleven minutes passed.

Haroun remained stretched out, with his eyes shut tight, concentrating.

A dark beam from the torch of a Chupwala searcher picked him out. The hisses of the search-party foamed across the waters. On their dark sea-horses, they galloped towards Butt the Hoopoe as fast as they could go.

And then, with a mighty shuddering and a mighty juddering, Haroun Khalifa's wish came true.

The Moon Kahani turned—quickly, because as Haroun had specified during his wishing, there was little time to be lost—and the sun rose, at high speed, and zoomed up into the sky until it was directly overhead; where it remained.

If Haroun had been in Gup City at that moment, he might have enjoyed witnessing the consternation of the Eggheads in P2C2E House. The immense super-computers and gigantic gyroscopes that had controlled the behaviour of the Moon, in order to preserve the Eternal Daylight and the Perpetual Darkness and the Twilight Strip in between, had simply gone crazy, and finally blown themselves apart. 'Whatever is doing this,' the Eggheads reported to the Walrus in consternation, 'possesses a force beyond our power to imagine, let alone control.'

But Haroun was not in Gup City—whose citizens had rushed open-mouthed into the streets, as night fell over Gup for the first time that anybody could remember, and the stars of the Milky Way Galaxy filled the sky. No, Haroun was on the back of Butt the Hoopoe, opening his eyes to find brilliant sunlight beating down on the waters of the Ocean and on the Dark Ship. 'What do you know?' he said. 'I did it! I actually managed to get it done.'

'Never doubted you for a moment,' replied Butt the Hoopoe without moving its beak. 'Move the whole Moon by will-power? Mister, I thought, *no problem*.'

Extraordinary things had begun to happen around them. The Chupwala searchers, racing towards Haroun on their dark sea-horses, began to shriek and hiss as the sunlight hit them; and then both Chupwalas and horses grew fuzzy at the edges, and began, as it seemed, to *melt* . . . into the poisoned, lethally acid Ocean they sank, turning into ordinary shadows, and then sizzling away altogether . . . 'Look,' yelled Haroun. 'Look what's happening to the ship!'

The sunlight had undone the black magic of the Cultmaster Khattam-Shud. Shadows could not remain solid in that brightness; and the huge ship itself had started to melt, had started losing its shape, as if it were a mountain of ice-cream left out in the sun by mistake.

'Iff! Mali!' shouted Haroun, and in spite of Butt's warnings he rushed up the gangway (which was becoming softer by the minute) towards the heaving deck.

~ ~ ~

By the time he reached the deck it was so sticky-soft that Haroun felt he was walking through fresh tar, or perhaps glue. Chupwala soldiers were screeching and rushing about madly, dissolving before Haroun's eyes into pools of shadow, and then vanishing altogether, because once the sorcery of Khattam-Shud had been destroyed by the sunlight, no shadow could survive without someone or something to be attached to, to be the shadow *of*. The Cultmaster, or to be precise his Shadow-Self, was nowhere to be seen.

Poison was evaporating from the cauldrons on deck; the cauldrons themselves were growing flabby and melting like dark butter. Even the gigantic crane, to which the Plug was attached by huge chains, was tilting and lolling in the shocking light of day.

The Water Genie and the Floating Gardener had been suspended over two of the poison-cauldrons by ropes which had been looped around their middles and then fastened to the smaller cranes that stood by each of the poison tanks. Just as Haroun spotted them, the ropes broke (they were woven out of shadows, too); and Iff and Mali plunged out of sight into the evil cauldrons. Haroun gave an anguished cry.

But the poison in the cauldrons had been boiled dry by the sun; and the cauldrons themselves had grown so soft that, as Haroun watched, Iff and Mali pulled away great sections with their bare hands, creating holes huge enough for them to step through. The cauldrons had been reduced to the consistency of melting cheese; and so had the deck itself. 'Let's get out of here,' Haroun suggested. The others followed him down the melting, rubbery gangway; Iff and Haroun leapt aboard Butt the Hoopoe, and Mali stepped on to the water beside them.

'Mission accomplished,' cried Haroun, joyfully. 'Hoopoe, full speed ahead!'

'Varoom,' agreed Butt the Hoopoe without moving its beak. It began moving rapidly away from the Dark Ship, towards the channel which Mali had cut in the weed-jungle; and then there was an unhealthy-sounding noise, and a slight smell of burning from the Hoopoe's brain-cavity, and they came to a halt.

'He's blown a fuse,' Iff pointed out. Haroun was mortified. 'I guess I didn't make the right connections after all,' he said. 'And I thought I'd been so good; now he's ruined, he'll never work again!'

'The great thing about a mechanical brain,' Iff consoled him, 'is that it can be fixed up, overhauled, even replaced. There's always a spare at the Service Station in Gup City. If we could get the Hoopoe back there, it would be as right as rain, hunky-dory, first class.'

'If we could get any of us back to anywhere,' Haroun said. They were adrift in the Old Zone, with no prospect of help. After everything they had been through, Haroun thought, it just didn't seem fair.

'I'll push for a while,' Mali offered, and had just begun to do so when, with a strange, sad, sucking sound, the Dark Ship of Cultmaster Khattam-Shud finally melted right away. And the Plug, incomplete as it was, fell harmlessly on to the ocean-bed, leaving the Source of Stories entirely unblocked-up. Fresh stories would go on pouring out of it, and so, one day, the Ocean would be clean again, and all the stories, even the oldest ones, would taste as good as new.

~ ~ ~

Mali could push them no further; he fell across the Hoopoe's back, exhausted. It was mid-afternoon now (the Moon Kahani had settled down to a 'normal' speed of rotation), and they drifted across the Southern Polar Ocean, not knowing what to do next.

Just then there was a bubbling and a frothing in the water beside them; and Haroun recognized, with immense relief, the many smiling mouths of the Plentimaw Fishes.

'Goopy! Bagha!' he greeted them happily. They replied:

'Have no worries! Have no fear!'

'We'll soon get you out of here!'

'You've done enough! Throw down the reins!'

'We'll soon have you safe again!'

So Bagha and Goopy, taking the reins of Butt the Hoopoe in their mouths, towed the companions out of the Old Zone. 'I wonder what became of Khattam-Shud,' Haroun finally said. Iff gave a contented shrug. 'Done for; I can vouch for that,' he said. 'No escape for the Cultmaster. He melted away like the rest of them. It's curtains for him, he's history, goodnight Charlie. I.e.: he's *khattam-shud.*'

'This was only the Shadow-Self, remember,' Haroun pointed out soberly. 'The other Cultmaster, the "real" one, is probably battling it out right now with General Kitab and the Pages, and Mudra, and my father—and Blabbermouth.' *Blabbermouth*, he thought privately. *I wonder if she missed me, just a little bit?*

What had been the Twilight Strip was now bathed in the last light of the sun. 'From now on, Kahani will be a sensible Moon,' Haroun thought, 'with sensible days and nights.' In the distance, to the north-east, he saw, lit up by the evening sun for the first time in many an age, the coastline of the Land of Chup.

11

Princess Batcheat

N ow I must tell you quickly about everything that happened while Haroun was away in the Old Zone:

Princess Batcheat Chattergy, you will remember, was being held prisoner in the topmost room of the topmost tower of the Citadel of Chup, the huge castle built entirely of black ice, which loomed over Chup City like an enormous Pterodactyl or Archaeopteryx. So it was to Chup City that the Guppee Army came, with General Kitab, Prince Bolo and Mudra the Shadow Warrior at its head.

Chup City was in the deep heart of the Perpetual Darkness, and the air was so cold that it would freeze into icicles on people's noses, and hang there until it was broken off. For this reason, the Chupwalas who lived there wore little spherical nosewarmers that gave them the look of circus clowns, except that the nosewarmers were black.

Red nosewarmers were issued to the Pages of Gup as they marched into the Darkness. 'Really, this is beginning to look like a war between buffoons,' thought Rashid the storyteller as he put on his false red nose. Prince Bolo, who found the things distinctly undignified, knew that a frozen, icicle-dangling nose would be even worse. So he sulked terribly but stuck his nosewarmer on as well.

Then there were the helmets. The Pages of Gup had been allocated the oddest headgear Rashid had ever seen (by courtesy of the Walrus and Eggheads back at P2C2E House). Around the rim of each helmet was a sort of hat-band that lit up brightly when the helmet was worn. This made the Pages of Gup look rather like a regiment of angels or saints, because they all had shining haloes around their

179

heads. The combined wattage of all these 'haloes' would just about enable the Guppees to see their opponents, even in the Perpetual Darkness; while the Chupwalas, even with their fashionable wrap-around dark glasses on, might be somewhat dazzled by the glare.

'This certainly is state-of-the-art warfare,' thought Rashid ironically. 'Neither army will even be able to see properly during the fight.'

Outside Chup City lay the battlefield, the wide plain of Bat-Mat-Karo, which had little hills at each end, where the rival commanders could pitch their tents and watch the battle's course. General Kitab, Prince Bolo and Mudra were joined on the Guppee command hill by Rashid the storyteller (who was needed, because only he could translate Mudra's Gesture Language to the others) and a detachment—or 'Pamphlet'—of Pages, including Blabbermouth, to act as messengers and guards. The Guppee commanders, all looking slightly silly in their red noses, sat down to a light pre-battle dinner in their tent; and while they were eating a Chupwala rode up to meet them, a little clerky fellow wearing, on his hooded cloak, the Sign of the Zipped Lips, and carrying a white flag of truce.

'Well, Chupwala,' said Prince Bolo dashingly and rather foolishly, 'what's your business? My, my,' he added, impolitely, 'what a measly, weasely, snivelling, drivelling sort of fellow you are.'

'Spots and fogs, Bolo,' boomed General Kitab, 'that's no way to address an ambassador who comes under a white flag.'

The ambassador gave an evil little grin of unconcern, and then spoke. 'The High Cultmaster, Khattam-Shud, has granted me special release from my vows of silence so that this message may be delivered,' he said in a low, hissing voice. 'He sends you greetings and informs you that you are all trespassing on the sacred soil of Chup. He will neither negotiate with you, nor give up your spying nosy-parker of a Batcheat. —And O, but she's noisy, too,' the ambassador added, clearly speaking for himself now. 'She torments our ears with her songs! And as for her nose, her teeth . . . '

'There's no need to go into that,' interrupted General Kitab. 'Drat it all! We aren't interested in your opinions. Complete your confounded message.'

The Chupwala ambassador cleared his throat. 'Khattam-Shud therefore warns you that, unless you retreat at once, your illegal invasion will be punished by annihilation; and Prince Bolo of Gup will be brought in chains to the Citadel, so that he may personally witness the Sewing-Up of Batcheat Chattergy's caterwauling mouth.'

'Knave, scoundrel, rapscallion, bounder, rogue!' shouted Prince Bolo. 'I should cut off your ears, have them sautéed in a little butter and garlic, and served to the hounds!'

'However,' continued the Chupwala ambassador, ignoring Bolo's outburst completely, 'before your utter defeat, I am commanded to entertain you for a moment, if you permit. I am, if I may immodestly say it, the finest juggler in Chup City; and am ordered to juggle, if you should so wish, for your delight.'

Blabbermouth, who was standing behind Prince Bolo's chair, here burst out: 'Don't *trust* him—it's a *trick* . . . '

General Kitab, with his love of argument, seemed perfectly willing to discuss this possibility, but Bolo waved a royal arm and cried, 'Silence, Page! The rules of chivalry demand our acceptance!' And to the Chupwala ambassador he said, as haughtily as he could manage: 'Fellow, we will see you juggle.'

The ambassador began his performance. From the depths of his cloak he produced a bewildering variety of objects—ebony balls, nine-pins, jade statuettes, porcelain tea-cups, live terrapins, lighted cigarettes, hats—and flung them into the air in mesmerizing hoops and whirls. The faster he juggled, the more complicated the juggling became; and his audience was so completely hypnotized by his skill that only one person in the tent saw the moment at which one extra object was added to the flying cavalcade, a little, heavy, rectangular box out of which protruded a short, burning fuse . . .

'Will you *for Pete's sake* look *out*?' yelled Blabbermouth, rushing forwards and sending Prince Bolo (and his chair) flying sideways. 'The guy's got a *live bomb*!'

She had reached the Chupwala ambassador in two strides, and, using her sharp eye and every ounce of her own juggling skills, she plucked the bomb right out of the rising, falling, dancing array of objects in the air. Other Pages seized the Chupwala, and statuettes and tea-cups and terrapins all plummeted to the ground . . . but Blabbermouth was rushing to the edge of the command hill as fast as her legs would carry her, and when she reached the edge she threw the bomb away down the hillside, where it exploded in an enormous (but now harmless) ball of glowing black flames.

The helmet had fallen from her head. Her long hair cascaded around her shoulders for all to see.

Bolo, the General, Mudra and Rashid rushed out of the tent when they heard the explosion. Blabbermouth was out of breath, but grinning happily. 'So, we *just about* got *that* in time,' she said. 'What a *creep* that Chupwala was. He was ready to *commit suicide*, to get blown up *right along with us*. I *told* you it was a trick.'

Prince Bolo, who didn't like his Pages to say 'I told you so', snapped back: 'What's this, Blabbermouth? Are you a girl?'

'You *noticed*, sire,' said Blabbermouth. 'No point *pretending* any *more*.'

'You tricked us,' said Bolo, blushing. 'You tricked *me*.'

Blabbermouth was outraged by Bolo's ingratitude. 'Tricking you isn't exactly *difficult*, excuse *me*,' she cried. '*Jugglers* can do it, so why not *girls*?'

Bolo went red in the face behind his red nosewarmer. 'You're fired,' he shouted at the top of his voice.

'Bolo, hang it all . . . ' began General Kitab.

'Oh, *no*, I'm *not*,' Blabbermouth shouted back. 'Mister, *I quit*.'

Mudra, the Shadow Warrior, had been observing these goings on with an utterly inscrutable expression on his green face. Now, however, his hands began to move, his legs to adopt eloquent positions, his facial muscles to ripple and twitch. Rashid translated: 'We must not quarrel when the battle is about to begin. If Prince Bolo has no further need of so courageous a Page, then perhaps Miss Blabbermouth would care to work for me?'

At which Prince Bolo of Gup looked crestfallen and ashamed, and Miss Blabbermouth looked exceptionally pleased.

~ ~ ~

The battle was joined at last.

Rashid Khalifa, watching the action from the Guppee command hill, was very much afraid that the Pages of Gup would be beaten badly. '*Torn up* would be the right term for Pages, I suppose,' he reflected, 'or perhaps *burned*.' His sudden capacity for bloodthirsty thoughts amazed him. 'I suppose war makes people crude,' he told himself.

The black-nosed Chupwala Army, whose menacing silence hung over it like a fog, looked too frightening to lose. Meanwhile the Guppees were still busily arguing over every little detail. Every order sent down from the command hill had to be debated fully, with all its pro's and con's, even if it came from General Kitab himself. 'How is it possible to fight a battle with all this chatter and natter?' Rashid wondered, perplexed.

But then the armies rushed at each other; and Rashid saw, to his great surprise, that the Chupwalas were quite unable to resist the Guppees. The Pages of Gup, now that they had talked through everything so fully, fought hard, remained united, supported each other when required to do so, and in general looked like a force with a common purpose. All those arguments and debates, all that openness, had created powerful bonds of fellowship between them. The Chupwalas, on the other hand, turned out to be a disunited rabble. Just as Mudra the Shadow Warrior had predicted, many of them actually had to fight their own, treacherous shadows! And as for the rest, well, their vows of silence and their habits of secrecy had made them suspicious and distrustful of one another. They had no faith in their generals, either. The upshot was that the Chupwalas did not stand shoulder to shoulder, but betrayed one another, stabbed one another in the back, mutinied, hid, deserted . . . and, after the shortest clash imaginable, simply threw down all their weapons and ran away.

~ ~ ~

After the Victory of Bat-Mat-Karo, the army or 'Library' of Gup entered Chup City in triumph. At the sight of Mudra, many Chupwalas threw in their lot with the Guppees. Chupwala maidens rushed black-nosed into the icy streets and garlanded the red-nosed and halo-headed Guppees with black snowdrops; and kissed them, too; and called them 'Liberators of Chup'.

Blabbermouth, her loose, flowing hair no longer concealed beneath velvet cap or halo-helmet, attracted the attention of several of the young lads of Chup City. But she stayed as close as she could to Mudra, as did Rashid Khalifa; and both Rashid and Blabbermouth found their thoughts turning constantly to Haroun. Where was he? Was he safe? When would he return?

Prince Bolo, who was out in front on his prancing mechanical horse, began to shout out in his habitual dashing but rather foolish way: 'Where are you, Khattam-Shud? Come out; your minions are defeated, and now it's your turn! Batcheat, never fear; Bolo is here! Where are you, Batcheat, my golden girl, my love? Batcheat, O Batcheat mine!'

'If you'd be quiet for a moment, you'd know soon enough where your Batcheat waits,' a Chupwala voice called out from the crowd that had gathered to greet the Guppees. (Many Chupwalas had started breaking the Laws of Silence now, cheering, shouting and so on.) 'Yes, use your ears,' a woman's voice agreed. 'Can't you hear that racket that's been driving us all to drink?'

'She sings?' Prince Bolo exclaimed, cupping a hand around an ear. 'My Batcheat sings? Then hush, friends, and hearken to her song.' He raised an arm. The Guppee parade came to a halt. And now, wafting down to them from the Citadel of Chup, came a woman's voice singing songs of love. It was the most horrible voice Rashid Khalifa, the Shah of Blah, had heard in all his life.

'If that's Batcheat,' he thought—but did not dare to say—'then you can almost understand why the Cultmaster wants to shut her up for good.'

> 'Oooh I'm talking 'bout my Bolo
> And I ain't got time for nothin' else,'

sang Batcheat, and glass shattered in shop windows. 'I'm sure I know that song, but the words seem different,' puzzled Rashid.

> 'Lemme tell you 'bout a boy I know,
> He's my Bolo and I love him so,'

sang Batcheat, and men and women in the crowd begged, 'No more! No more!' Rashid frowned, and shook his head: 'Yes, yes, it's very familiar, too, but not exactly right.'

> 'He won't play polo,
> He can't fly solo,
> Oo-wee but I love him true,
> Our love will grow-lo,
> I'll never let him go-lo,
> Got those waiting-for-my-Bolo
> Blues,'

sang Batcheat, and Prince Bolo shouted, 'Beautiful! That's so beautiful!'—to which the crowd of Chupwalas rejoined, 'Aargghh, somebody stop her, please.'

> 'His name ain't Rollo,
> His voice ain't low-lo,
> Uh-huh but I love him fine,
> So stop the show-lo,
> Pay me what you owe-lo,
> I'm gonna make that Bolo
> Mine,'

sang Batcheat, and Prince Bolo, cavorting on his horse, almost swooned with delight. 'Just listen to that,' he rhapsodized. 'Is that a voice, or what is it?'

'It must be a what-is-it,' the crowd shouted back, 'because a voice it is certainly not.'

Prince Bolo was deeply miffed. 'These persons obviously cannot appreciate fine contemporary singing,' he said loudly to General Kitab and Mudra. 'So I think we should attack the Citadel now, if you don't mind.'

At that moment a miracle happened.

The ground shook beneath their feet: once, twice, thrice. The houses of Chup City trembled; many Chupwalas (and Guppees, too) cried out in terror. Prince Bolo fell off his horse.

'An earthquake, an earthquake!' people shouted—but it was no ordinary earthquake. It was the entire Moon, Kahani, with a mighty shuddering and a mighty juddering, spinning on its axis, towards the . . .

'Look at the sky!' voices were shouting. 'Look what's coming up over the horizon!'

. . . towards the sun.

The sun was rising over Chup City, over the Citadel of Chup. It was rising rapidly, and went on rising until it was directly overhead, blazing down in the full fury of its noonday heat; and there it stayed. Many Chupwalas, including Mudra, the Shadow Warrior, took really rather fashionable wrap-around dark glasses out of their pockets, and put them on.

Sunrise! It tore away the shrouds of silence and shadow

which the sorcery of Khattam-Shud had hung around the Citadel. The black ice of that dark fortress received the sunlight like a mortal wound.

The locks on the Citadel gates melted away. Prince Bolo, with drawn sword, galloped through the opened gates, followed by Mudra and several 'Chapters' of Pages.

'Batcheat!' Bolo shouted as he charged. His horse whinnied at the name.

'Bolo!' came the faraway reply.

Bolo dismounted; and with Mudra ran up flights of stairs, and through courtyards, and up yet more staircases, while all around him the pillars of Khattam-Shud's Citadel, softened by the sun's heat, began to buckle and bend. Arches were drooping, cupolas melting. The shadowless servants of the Cultmaster, the members of the Union of the Zipped Lips, were running blindly hither and yon, smashing into walls, knocking one another out as they collided, and shrieking dreadfully, all Laws of Silence forgotten in their fear.

It was the moment of Khattam-Shud's final destruction. As Bolo and the Shadow Warrior leapt upwards into the melting heart of the Citadel, the Prince's cries of 'Batcheat!' brought walls and towers tumbling down. And at last, just as they were despairing about her safety, the Princess Batcheat came into sight, with that nose (in a black Chupwala nosewarmer), those teeth . . . but there's no need to go into that. Let's just say there was no question but that it was indeed Batcheat, followed by her handmaidens, sliding down towards them along the banister of a grand staircase whose steps had melted away. Bolo waited; Batcheat flew off the banister into his arms. He staggered backwards, but did not fall.

Now the air was full of a great groaning noise. As Bolo, Batcheat, Mudra and the handmaidens fled down, down, through soggy courtyards and down squashy staircases, they looked back; and saw, high above them, at the very apex of the Citadel, the gigantic ice-statue, the colossal ice-idol of tongueless, grinning, many-toothed Bezaban beginning to totter and shake; and then, drunkenly, it fell.

It was like the fall of a mountain. What remained of the halls and courtyards of the Citadel of Chup was utterly smashed as Bezaban crashed down. The statue's huge head snapped off at the neck and came rolling and bouncing down the terraces of the Citadel, towards the lowest courtyard, where Bolo, Mudra and the ladies now stood, at the Citadel's gates, watching these events with fascinated horror, with Rashid Khalifa, General Kitab, and a great host of Guppees and Chupwalas gathered at their backs.

Down and down the great head bounced; its ears, its nose broke off as it hit the ground; the teeth fell from its mouth. Down and down it came. Then, 'Look!' shouted Rashid Khalifa, pointing; and a moment later, 'Look out!' He had seen an unimpressive little figure in a hooded cloak come scurrying out into this lowest courtyard of the Citadel: a skinny, scrawny, snivelling, drivelling, mingy, stingy, measly, weaselly, clerkish sort of fellow, who had no shadow but seemed almost as much a shadow as a man. It was the Cultmaster, Khattam-Shud, running for his life. He heard Rashid's cry too late; whirled around with a fiendish yell;

and saw the huge head of the Colossus of Bezaban as it arrived, hitting him squarely on the nose. It crushed him to bits; not a shred of him was ever seen again. The head, grinning toothlessly, sat in that courtyard and continued, slowly, to melt.

~ ~ ~

Peace broke out.

The new government of the Land of Chup, headed by Mudra, announced its desire for a long and lasting peace with Gup, a peace in which Night and Day, Speech and Silence, would no longer be separated into Zones by Twilight Strips and Walls of Force.

Mudra invited Miss Blabbermouth to stay with him, to learn the Gesture Language Abhinaya, so that she might act as go-between for the Guppee authorities and those of Chup; and Blabbermouth accepted gladly.

In the meanwhile, Guppee Water Genies on flying mechanical birds were sent to search the Ocean, and after a short time they located the incapacitated Hoopoe, being drawn north by Goopy and Bagha, with three exhausted but happy 'spies' upon its back.

Haroun was reunited with his father, and with Blabbermouth, who seemed oddly awkward and shy in his presence, which was more or less how he felt in hers. They met on the shores of Chup in what had been the Twilight Strip; and everyone set off contentedly for Gup City, because there was a marriage to arrange.

191

Back in Gup City, the Speaker of the Chatterbox announced certain promotions: Iff was named Chief Water Genie; Mali was named Head Floating Gardener; and Goopy and Bagha were appointed Leaders of all the Plentimaw Fishes in the Sea. These four were given the joint responsibility for the very large Cleaning-Up operation which was to begin at once across the length and breadth of the Ocean of the Streams of Story. They announced that they were especially anxious to restore the Old Zone as soon as possible, so that these ancient tales could be fresh and new once more.

Rashid Khalifa was given back his Story Water facilities, and awarded the Land of Gup's highest decoration, the Order of the Open Mouth, in recognition of his exceptional services during the war. The newly appointed Chief Water Genie agreed to reconnect Rashid's water supply personally.

Butt the Hoopoe was quickly restored to its normal self, just as soon as the Gup Service Station had fitted it with its spare brain.

And Princess Batcheat? She had survived her imprisonment unharmed, although her fear of having her mouth sewn up had left her with a hatred of needles that would last her whole life. And on the day of her wedding to Prince Bolo, the two of them looked so happy and so much in love as they stood on the palace balcony waving to the crowd of Guppees and visiting Chupwalas gathered below, that everyone decided to forget about how incredibly idiotic Batcheat had been to get herself captured in the first place, and about Bolo's many pieces of foolish behaviour during the war that followed. 'After all,' Iff the Chief Water Genie whispered to Haroun as they stood together on the balcony, a little way from the happy couple, 'it's not as if we really let our crowned heads do anything very important around here.'

'A great victory has been won,' old King Chattergy was saying to the crowd, 'a victory for our Ocean over its Enemy, but also a victory for the new Friendship and Openness between Chup and Gup, over our old Hostility and Suspicion. A dialogue has been opened; and to celebrate that, as well as this wedding, let all the people sing.'

'Even better,' suggested Bolo, 'let Batcheat serenade us—let her golden voice be heard!'

There was a brief silence. Then, with one voice, the crowd roared: 'No, not that—spare us that, if you please.'

Batcheat and Bolo both looked so hurt that it was necessary for old King Chattergy to save the day by saying, soothingly: 'What the people mean is that, on your wedding day, they wish to show their love by singing to you.' Which was not precisely true, but it cheered the couple up; and then the square was full of song. Batcheat kept her mouth shut, and everyone was as happy as could be.

As he left the balcony behind the royal party, Haroun was approached by an Egghead. 'You're to present yourself at once at P2C2E House,' the Egghead said coldly. 'The Walrus wants to talk to the person who destroyed so much irreplaceable machinery so wilfully.'

'But it was in a good cause,' Haroun protested. The Egghead shrugged. 'I don't know about that,' he said as he walked off. 'That's for you to argue and the Walrus to decide.'

12

Was It the Walrus?

'What I need is witnesses,' Haroun decided. 'Once Iff and Mali tell the Walrus why I had to make my wish, he'll understand about his broken machinery.' A wild party was getting under way in the royal palace, and it took Haroun a few minutes to find the Chief Water Genie in the balloon-popping, rice-throwing, streamer-waving throng. He finally located Iff, whose turban was a little askew, dancing frenziedly with a young woman Genie. Haroun had to shout to make himself heard over the music and general hubbub; and then, to his horror, he saw Iff purse his lips and shake his head. 'Sorry,' said the Chief Water Genie. 'Argue with the Walrus? Not worth the candle, include me out, no can do.'

'But, Iff, you've got to,' Haroun pleaded. 'Somebody has to explain!'

'Explanations not my forte,' Iff yelled back. 'Not my long suit, I'm no good at them, not my thing at all.'

Haroun rolled his eyes in frustration, and went in search of Mali. He found the Head Floating Gardener at the second wedding party, which was being held on (and under) the Lagoon, for the benefit of those Guppees (the Plentimaw Fishes and the Floating Gardeners) who preferred a watery setting. Mali was easy to spot: he was standing on the back of Butt the Hoopoe, with his hat of weeds tilted at a jaunty angle, and he was singing lustily to an enthusiastic audience of Fishes and Gardeners:

> You can melt Dark Ships,
> You can melt what's shadowee,

197

You can melt Ice Castles, but
You can't melt me!

'Mali,' called Haroun. 'Help!'

The Head Floating Gardener broke off his song, took off his hat of weeds, scratched his head, and said through his floral lips: 'Walrus. You're on the carpet. Heard all about it. Big problem. Sorry, can't assist.'

'What's the matter with everybody?' cried Haroun. 'What's so scary about this Walrus, anyway? He seemed okay when I met him before, even if his moustache wasn't really very like a walrus moustache.'

Mali shook his head sadly. 'Walrus. Important fellow. Wouldn't like to get on the wrong side of him. You take my meaning.'

'Oh, honestly,' Haroun shouted, crossly. 'I'll just have to go and face the music alone. Some friends!'

'No point even asking me, which you didn't,' Butt the Hoopoe called after him without moving its beak. 'I'm only a machine.'

As Haroun passed through the huge doors of P2C2E House, his heart sank. He stood in the vast, echoing entrance hall as white-coated Eggheads walked rapidly past him in every direction. Haroun fancied that they all eyed him with a mixture of anger, contempt, and pity. He had to ask three Eggheads the way to the Walrus's office before he finally found it, after mazy wanderings around P2C2E House that reminded him of following Blabbermouth around the palace. At last, however, he was standing in front of a golden door on which were written the words: GRAND COMPTROLLER OF PROCESSES TOO COMPLICATED TO EXPLAIN. I. M. D. WALRUS, ESQUIRE. KNOCK AND WAIT.

'Here I am at last, about to get the interview for which I came to Kahani in the first place,' Haroun reflected nervously. 'But it wasn't supposed to be this sort of an interview at all.' He took a deep breath; and knocked.

The Walrus's voice called: 'Come in.' Haroun took another breath and opened the door.

The first thing he saw was the Walrus, sitting on a shiny white chair at a shiny yellow desk, with his large, hairless, egg-shaped head shining as brightly as the furniture, and the moustache on his upper lip twitching feverishly in what could easily have been anger.

The second thing Haroun noticed was that the Walrus was not alone.

In the Walrus's office, grinning broadly, were King Chattergy, Prince Bolo, Princess Batcheat, the Speaker of the Chatterbox, President Mudra of Chup, his aide Miss Blabbermouth, General Kitab, Iff, Mali, and Rashid Khalifa, too. On the wall was a video monitor on which Haroun saw Goopy and Bagha grinning at him from under the Lagoon's surface, grinning with every one of their mouths. Butt the Hoopoe's head stared out at him from a second such monitor.

Haroun was flabbergasted. 'Am I in trouble or not?' he managed to inquire. Everybody in the room burst into laughter. 'You must forgive us,' the Walrus said, wiping tears of laughter from his eyes, and still giggling slightly. 'We were pulling your leg. Just our little yolk. Little *yolk*,' he repeated, and burst out laughing all over again.

'Then what's this all about?' Haroun asked. The Walrus pulled himself together and put on his most serious face, which would have been fine except that he then caught Iff's eye and that set him off laughing again; and that set Iff off again; and that set everyone else off. It was several minutes before order returned.

'Haroun Khalifa,' said the Walrus, getting to his feet, still slightly out of breath and holding his aching sides, 'to honour you for the incalculable service you have done to the peoples of Kahani and to the Ocean of the Streams of Story, we grant you the right to ask of us whatever favour you desire, and we promise to grant it if we possibly can, even if it means inventing a brand-new Process Too Complicated To Explain.'

Haroun was silent.

'Well, Haroun,' asked Rashid, 'any ideas?'

Haroun was silent again, looking suddenly unhappy. It was Blabbermouth who understood his mood, and came over to him, took his hand and asked, 'What is it? What's the matter?'

'It's no use asking for anything,' Haroun answered in a low voice, 'because what I really want is something nobody here can give me.'

'Nonsense,' retorted the Walrus. 'I know perfectly well what you want. You've been on a great adventure, and at the end of great adventures everybody wants the same thing.'

'Oh? And what's that?' asked Haroun, a little belligerently.

'A happy ending,' the Walrus said. That shut Haroun up. 'Isn't it the truth?' the Walrus pressed him.

'Well, yes, I suppose it is,' Haroun admitted, uncomfortably. 'But the happy ending I'm thinking of isn't something you can find in any Sea, even a Sea with Plentimaw Fishes in it.'

The Walrus nodded slowly and judiciously, seven times. Then he put his finger-tips together and sat down at his desk, motioning to Haroun and the rest that they should be seated, too. Haroun sat in a shiny white chair facing the Walrus across the desk; the others sat in similar chairs that were lined up against the walls.

'Ahem,' the Walrus began. 'Happy endings are much rarer in stories, and also in life, than most people think. You could almost say they are the exceptions, not the rule.'

'You agree with me, then,' said Haroun. 'So that's that.'

'It is precisely because happy endings are so rare,' the Walrus continued, 'that we at P2C2E House have learnt how to synthesize them artificially. In plain language: *we can make them up.*'

'That's impossible,' Haroun protested. 'They aren't things you can put in bottles.' But then he added, uncertainly: 'Are they?'

'If Khattam-Shud could synthesize anti-stories,' said the Walrus with just a hint of injured pride, 'I should think you'd accept that we can synthesize things, too. As for "impossible,"' he went on, 'most people would say that everything that's happened to you lately is quite, quite impossible. Why make a fuss about this particular impossible thing?'

There was a further silence.

'Very well, then,' Haroun said boldly. 'You said it could be a big wish, and so it is. I come from a sad city, a city so sad that it has forgotten its name. I want you to provide a happy ending, not just for my adventure, but for the whole sad city as well.'

'Happy endings must come at the end of something,' the Walrus pointed out. 'If they happen in the middle of a story, or an adventure, or the like, all they do is cheer things up for a while.'

'That'll do,' said Haroun.

Then it was time to go home.

~ ~ ~

They went quickly, because Haroun hated long goodbyes. Saying goodbye to Blabbermouth proved particularly difficult, and if she hadn't leant forward without warning and kissed him, Haroun would probably never have found a way of kissing her; but when it was done, he found he wasn't embarrassed in the least, but felt extremely pleased; which made it even harder to leave.

At the foot of the Pleasure Garden, Haroun and Rashid waved goodbye to their friends and climbed, with Iff, on to the back of Butt the Hoopoe. Only now did it occur to Haroun that Rashid must have missed his storytelling appointment in K, and so, no doubt, an angry Snooty

Buttoo would be waiting for them when they returned to the Dull Lake. 'But but but never mind,' Butt the Hoopoe said without moving its beak. 'When you travel with Butt the Hoopoe, time is on your side. Leave late, arrive early! Let's go! Va-voom-varoom!'

Night had fallen over the Dull Lake. Haroun saw the houseboat, *Arabian Nights Plus One*, lying peacefully at anchor in the moonlight. They landed by an open bedroom window, and as Haroun climbed in he was overwhelmed by fatigue, and there was nothing for it but to flop into his peacock bed and go straight to sleep.

When he awoke it was a bright, sunny morning. Everything seemed as it had always been; of flying mechanical Hoopoes and Water Genies there was no trace.

He got up, rubbing his eyes, and found Rashid Khalifa sitting on the little balcony at the front of the houseboat, still in his long blue nightshirt, sipping a cup of tea. A boat in the shape of a swan was coming towards them across the Lake.

'I had such a strange dream . . .' Rashid Khalifa began, but he was interrupted by the voice of Snooty Buttoo, who was waving energetically from the swan-boat: 'Hoo! Halloo!' called Mr Buttoo.

'Oh, Lord,' thought Haroun. 'Now there will be screaming and shouting and we'll have to pay our own bill.'

'Hoo, somnolent Mr Rashid!' called Buttoo. 'Can it be that you and your son are still in your nightshirts, when I am coming to fetch you for the show? Crowds are waiting, tardy Mr Rashid! I trust you will not disappoint.'

It seemed that the entire adventure of Kahani had passed off in less than a single night! 'But that's impossible,' thought Haroun; which made him remember the Walrus asking, 'Why make a fuss about this particular impossible thing?'—and so he turned urgently to his father and asked, 'Your dream—can you recall it?'

'Not now, Haroun,' said Rashid Khalifa, who then called over to the approaching Mr Buttoo: 'Why so anxious, sir? Come aboard, take tea, we will quickly dress and be off.' To Haroun he said, 'Look sharp, son. The Shah of Blah is never late. The Ocean of Notions has a reputation for punctuality to preserve.'

'The Ocean,' Haroun urged, as Buttoo drew near in the swan-boat. 'Please think. It's very important.' But Rashid wasn't listening at all.

Haroun went off somewhat disconsolately to get dressed; and now he noticed a little golden envelope lying by his pillow, an envelope of the type in which grand hotels sometimes leave night-time mint chocolates for their guests. Inside it was a note written by Blabbermouth and signed by her, and by all his friends from the Moon Kahani. (Goopy and Bagha, who couldn't write, had placed fishy lips upon the paper, sending kisses instead of signatures.)

'Come whenever you want,' the note said. 'Stay as long as you like. Remember: when you fly with Butt the Hoopoe, time is on your side.'

There was something else in the golden envelope: a tiny bird, perfect in every detail, cocking its head up at him. It was, of course, the Hoopoe.

'That wash and brush-up certainly did you a world of good,' Rashid said as Haroun emerged from his room. 'I haven't seen you looking so pleased with life for months.'

~ ~ ~

You'll recall that Mr Buttoo and his unpopular local government were expecting Rashid Khalifa to win them the people's support by telling 'up-beat, praising sagas' and cutting out the 'gloompuss yarns'. They had decked out a large park with every sort of happy decoration—bunting, streamers, flags—and they had put loudspeakers on poles all over the park, so that everyone could hear the Shah of Blah properly. There was a colourful stage plastered with posters that said VOTE BUTTOO, or, alternatively, WHO'S THE ONE FOR YOU?—NOT JUST ONE, BUTTOO! And a large crowd had indeed gathered to hear Rashid; but from their scowling expressions Haroun gathered that the people didn't care for Mr Buttoo at all.

'You're on,' snapped Mr Buttoo. 'Much-praised Mr Rashid, you'd better be good; or else.'

Haroun watched from the side of the stage as Rashid went smiling to the microphone amid generous applause. Then he gave Haroun a real shock, because his first words were, 'Ladies and gentlemen, the name of the tale I am going to tell is *Haroun and the Sea of Stories*.'

'So you didn't forget,' Haroun thought with a smile.

Rashid Khalifa, the Ocean of Notions, the Shah of Blah, looked across to his son and winked. *Did you think I'd forget a story like this one?* said the wink. Then he began:

'There was once, in the country of Alifbay, a sad city, the saddest of cities, a city so ruinously sad that it had forgotten its name.'

~ ~ ~

As you will have guessed, Rashid told the people in that park the same story I've just told you. Haroun decided his father must have asked Iff and the others about the bits at which he hadn't personally been present, because his account of them was so accurate. And it was plain that he was okay again, the Gift of the Gab had returned, and he had the audience right in the palm of his hand. When he sang Mali's songs they all sang along, 'You can chop suey, but you can't chop me,' and when he sang Batcheat's songs they begged for mercy.

Whenever Rashid was talking about Khattam-Shud and his henchmen from the Union of the Zipped Lips, the whole audience stared very hard at Snooty Buttoo and *his* henchmen, who were sitting behind Rashid on the stage, looking less and less happy as the story unfolded. And when Rashid told the audience how almost all the Chupwalas had hated the Cultmaster all along, but had been afraid to say so, well, then a loud murmur of sympathy for the Chupwalas ran through the crowd, *yes*, people muttered, *we know exactly how they felt*. And after the two falls of the two Khattam-Shuds, somebody started up a chant of, 'Mister Buttoo—go for good; Mister Buttoo—*khattam-shud*,' and the entire audience joined in. On hearing this chant, Snooty

Buttoo understood that the game was up, and went slinking with his henchmen off the stage. The crowd allowed him to escape, but pelted him with rubbish as he fled. Mr Buttoo was never seen again in the Valley of K, which left the people of the Valley free to choose leaders they actually liked.

'Of course, we didn't get paid,' Rashid told Haroun cheerfully as they waited for the Mail Coach to take them out of the Valley. 'But never mind; money isn't everything.'

'But but but,' said a familiar voice from the driver's seat of the Mail Coach, 'no money is nothing at all.'

~ ~ ~

It was still raining cats and dogs when they returned to the sad city. Many of the streets were flooded. 'Who cares?' Rashid Khalifa cried gaily. 'Let's walk home. I haven't had a good soaking in years.'

Haroun had been worried that Rashid would be depressed about returning to the apartment full of broken clocks and no Soraya, so he gave his father a suspicious look. But Rashid skipped out into the wet, and the wetter he got, as they walked through shin-deep muddy water, the more boyishly happy he became. Haroun began to catch his father's good mood, and soon the two of them were splashing and chasing each other like little children.

After a while Haroun noticed that, as a matter of fact, the city streets were full of people fooling around in the same way, running and jumping and splashing and falling and, above all, laughing their heads off.

'Looks like this old city finally learnt how to have fun,' Rashid grinned.

'But why?' Haroun asked. 'Nothing's really changed, has it? Look, the sadness factories are still in production, you can see the smoke; and almost everybody is still poor . . . '

'Hey, you, long-face,' shouted an elderly gent who must have been at least seventy years old, but who was dancing through the flooded, rainy streets, waving a rolled umbrella like a sword. 'Don't you sing those Tragedy Songs round here.'

Rashid Khalifa approached this gentleman. 'We've been out of town, sir,' he said. 'Has something happened while we've been away? A miracle, for example?'

'It's just the rain,' replied the old bird. 'It's making everybody happy. Me, included. Whee! Whoopee!' And he skipped away down the road.

'It's the Walrus,' Haroun realized suddenly. 'It's the Walrus, making my wish come true. There must be artificial happy endings mixed up with the rain.'

'If it is the Walrus,' said Rashid, doing a little jig in a puddle, 'then the city owes you a big vote of thanks.'

'Don't, Dad,' said Haroun, his good mood deflating all at once. 'Don't you get it? It isn't real. It's just something the Eggheads got out of a bottle. It's all fake. People should be happy when there's something to be happy about, not just when they get bottled happiness poured over them from the sky.'

'I'll tell you what to be happy about,' said a policeman who chanced to be floating by on an upturned umbrella. 'We remembered the city's name.'

'Well, out with it, tell us quickly,' Rashid insisted, feeling very excited.

'Kahani,' said the policeman brightly as he floated off down the flooded street. 'Isn't it a beautiful name for a city? It means "story", you know.'

~ ~ ~

They turned into their own lane, and saw their house, looking like a soggy cake in the rain. Rashid was still hopping and bounding gaily along, but Haroun's feet grew heavier with each step; he was finding his father's cheerfulness simply unbearable, and he blamed the Walrus for it all, for everything, for all that was bad and wrong and fake in the whole wide motherless world.

Miss Oneeta came out on to her upstairs balcony. 'O, too fine, you are returned! Come, come, what sweets and celebrations we will have!' She was wobbling and bobbling and clapping her hands for joy.

'What is there to celebrate?' Haroun demanded as Miss Oneeta came scurrying down to join him and his father in the rainy street.

'To speak personally,' Miss Oneeta replied, 'I have said good-riddance to Mr Sengupta. And I also have a job, in the chocolate factory, and as many chocolates as I require are free of charge. And also I have several admirers—but listen to me, how shameless, talking like this to you!'

'I'm happy for you,' Haroun replied. 'But in our life it is not all songs and dances.'

Miss Oneeta put on a mysterious expression. 'Maybe you

have been away too long,' she said. 'Things change.'

This made Rashid frown. 'Oneeta, what are you talking about? If you have something to tell . . . '

The front door of the Khalifa apartment opened, and there stood Soraya Khalifa, as large as life and twice as beautiful. Haroun and Rashid couldn't move. They stayed frozen like statues in the pouring rain with their mouths hanging open.

'Was this the Walrus's work, too?' Rashid murmured to Haroun, who just shook his head. Rashid answered himself: 'Who knows? Maybe so and maybe no, as our friend the Mail Coach driver would say.'

Soraya had come out to join them in the rain. 'What Walrus?' she asked. 'I don't know any Walrus, but I know that I made a mistake. I went; I don't deny. I went, but now, if you want, then I am back.'

Haroun looked at his father. Rashid couldn't speak.

'That Sengupta, I swear,' Soraya went on. 'What a skinny, scrawny, snivelling, drivelling, mingy, stingy, measly, weaselly clerk! As far as I'm concerned he's finished with, done for, gone for good.'

'*Khattam-shud*,' Haroun said quietly.

'That's right,' his mother answered. 'I promise. Mr Sengupta is *khattam-shud*.'

'Welcome home,' Rashid said, and the three Khalifas (and Miss Oneeta, too) fell into one another's arms.

'Come inside,' Soraya suggested eventually. 'There is a limit to how much rain a person can enjoy.'

~ ~ ~

That night, when he went to bed, Haroun took the miniaturized Butt the Hoopoe out of its little golden envelope and put it on the palm of his left hand. 'Please understand,' he said to the Hoopoe, 'it's really good to know you'll be here when I need you. But the way things are just now, I honestly don't need to go anywhere at all.'

'But but but,' said the miniaturized Hoopoe in a miniaturized voice (and without moving its beak), 'no problem.'

Haroun put Butt the Hoopoe back in its envelope, put the envelope under his pillow, put the pillow under his head and fell asleep.

When he woke up there were new clothes laid out at the foot of his bed, and on his bedside table was a new clock, fully operational, and telling the right time. 'Presents?' he wondered. 'What's all this?'

Then he remembered: it was his birthday. He could hear his mother and father moving about in the apartment, waiting for him to emerge. He got up, dressed in his new clothes, and took a closer look at his new clock.

'Yes,' he nodded to himself, 'time is definitely on the move again around these parts.'

Outside, in the living room, his mother had begun to sing.

The End

About the Names in this Book

any of the names given to people and places in this story have been derived from Hindustani words.

Abhinaya is, in fact, the name of the Language of Gesture used in Indian classical dance.

Alifbay is an imaginary country. Its name comes from the Hindustani word for 'alphabet'.

Batcheat is from 'baat-cheet', that is, 'chit-chat'.

Bat-Mat-Karo means 'Do-Not-Speak'.

Bezaban means 'Without-a-Tongue'.

Bolo comes from the verb 'bolna', to speak. 'Bolo!' is the imperative: 'Speak!'

Chup (pronounce the 'u' like the 'oo' in 'good') means 'quiet'; '**Chupwala**' means something like 'quiet fellow'.

The Dull Lake, which doesn't exist, gets its name from the Dal Lake in Kashmir, which does.

Goopy and **Bagha** don't mean anything special, but they are also the names of the two goofy heroes of a movie by Satyajit Ray. The movie characters are not fishes, but they are pretty fishy.

Gup (pronounce the 'u' as in 'cup') means 'gossip'. It can also mean 'nonsense' or 'fib'.

Haroun and **Rashid** are both named after the legendary Caliph of Baghdad, Haroun al-Rashid, who features in many Arabian Nights tales. Their surname, **Khalifa**, actually means 'Caliph'.

Kahani means 'story'.

Khamosh means 'silent'.

Khattam-Shud means 'completely finished', 'over and done with'.

Kitab means 'book'.

Mali, not surprisingly, means 'gardener'.

Mudra, who speaks Abhinaya, the Language of Gesture (see above), is also named after it, in a way. A 'mudra' is any one of the gestures that make up the language.